McCOMB PUBLIC LIBRARY
McCOMB, OHIO

D1527919

Praise for the Kindred series

Mountain Laurel

"*Mountain Laurel* is the sort of book where you really hope there will be a sequel because you want to spend more time with the characters. It's a fascinating story, rich in emotion and a sense of the time and cultures in which it takes place."

DIANA GABALDON, *New York Times* bestselling author of the Outlander series

"Lori Benton is an extraordinary storyteller. She invites her readers into the 1790s of the Carolinas, where every character and plot twist speaks of bondage and freedom, kin and courage, choice and consequence. Every page delivers a unique, satisfying, and enriching read, where faith and family exposes and nurtures the journey of the human heart."

JANE KIRKPATRICK, *New York Times* bestselling author of *Something Worth Doing*

"Poignant. Impeccably researched. Tender and romantic but with a powerful message of clinging to faith over fear, *Mountain Laurel* is Lori Benton at her finest. An expertly woven eighteenth-century story line with topics of freedom, family, and characters grappling over intense choices—with potentially life-altering consequences—makes this a novel that is just as relevant in our world today. This is a stellar series debut!"

KRISTY CAMBRON, bestselling author of *The Butterfly and the Violin* and *The Lost Castle*

Shiloh

"In a sweeping saga swelling with soul, *Shiloh* carries the beloved characters of *Mountain Laurel* and *Burning Sky* into a stirring and masterfully woven conclusion with a theme that resounds through the ages: restoration. Lori Benton dares to write characters whose lives are nuanced, complex, even cracked in tender wounds . . . and through those cracks, within the pages of *Shiloh*, something beautiful shines: the light of hope . . . a tale not to be missed!"

AMANDA DYKES, author of *Yours is the Night, Set the Stars Alight*, and the 2020 Christy Award-winning *Whose Waves These Are*

"Lori Benton's latest is a rich tapestry of lost love and betrayal, of heartache and compassion—and ultimately, of redemption and restoration. The courage and resilience of the human spirit is woven through every page of this highly enjoyable novel."

TAMERA ALEXANDER, USA Today bestselling author of *Colors of Truth*, a Carnton novel

"A sumptuous tale, so true to life you will hope and yearn and dare to dream along with Ian and Seona as they wrestle with what reconciliation and second chances really mean. Lori Benton delivers another impeccably-researched historical that kept me up late turning pages and haunted my thoughts when I reached the end."

LAURA FRANTZ, Christy Award-winning author of *A Heart Adrift*

"An absolute triumph! With nuance and sensitivity, this tale explores the complexities of life after freedom from bondage. It's a landscape of hope, fear, choices, love, surrender, and ultimately, victory over that which ensnares."

JOCELYN GREEN, Christy Award-winning author of *Between Two Shores* and *Shadows of the White City*

Books by Lori Benton

Connected to this novella:

BURNING SKY (Willa, Neil, and Joseph Tames-His-Horse's story)

THE PURSUIT OF TAMSEN LITTLEJOHN (Cade, Jesse, Tamsen, and Ambrose Kincaid's story)

MANY SPARROWS (Jeremiah Ring's story)

THE KING'S MERCY (Joanna, Jemma, Runs-Far, and Alex MacKinnon's story)

The Kindred series

1: MOUNTAIN LAUREL (Ian Cameron, Seona, Lily, Thomas, and Esther's story)

2: SHILOH (Ian and Seona's story continued)

3. THE JOURNEY OF RUNS-FAR, a Kindred novella (this story)

Independent of this novella:

The Pathfinders

1: THE WOOD'S EDGE

2: A FLIGHT OF ARROWS

The Journey of Runs-Far

A Kindred Novella

Lori Benton

Author of Mountain Laurel
And Shiloh

The Journey of Runs-Far, a Kindred novella
© 2021 by Lori Benton

Published in association with the Books & Such Literary Management, 52 Mission Circle, Suite 122, PMB 170, Santa Rosa, CA 95409-5370, www.booksandsuch.com.

All characters and events in this book are fictitious. Any resemblance to actual persons, living or dead, or to actual events is purely coincidental.

All rights reserved. No part of this publication may be reproduced, stored in a retrieval system, or transmitted in any form or by any means—electronic, mechanical, photocopy, recording or any other—except for brief quotations in printed reviews without the written prior permission of the publisher.

Print ISBN: 9798463094551

Printed in the United States of America
15 14 13 12 10 9 8 7 6 5 4 3 2 1

To my Yadas, near and far—
Karen, Linda, Sarah, Hannah, Patti, Stacy, Fiona, Sandy, Bonnie, Ann, Chelsea, Maxine, Andi, Connie, Jennifer, & DJ
—for taking my hand in this dance.

Prologue

Kagali — Bone Moon
(February 1798)

THUNDER-GOING-AWAY'S TOWN

Outside the lodge snow was melting, muddying village footpaths. Inside a fire blazed, warding off the cold. In a nest of blankets near the fire's warmth lay a beloved elder, who was dying.

At least that was what everyone assumed that elder was doing—had been doing for days. Long enough that all who wished to bid him farewell had been sent for. Many had come, some from beyond the high, sheltering blue mountains the elder called home, to slip by twos and threes into the lodge where he and his son were living. Or in the elder's case, dying.

This man, who some called Timothy, had years ago gone back to thinking of himself as Runs-Far, the name his mother's Longhair Clan gave him as a boy who, not surprisingly, loved to run. *Timothy* was the name given when, not yet blooded in battle, he had prayed with a holy man, repented of sin, and become a Jesus-follower. It was long since he felt he merited that name. Now he was dying.

Runs-Far had first observed death stalking him in midwinter. Having seen sixty-six winters did not make him terribly old, yet he had not prayed to be delivered. With more relief than regret he had turned to watch death creeping up on him like a panther before it springs.

Lying in the blankets now, eyes fast shut and unaware of the people gathered, Runs-Far had stopped thinking about dying. He was thinking, or maybe dreaming, of Walnut, the wife of his youth, taken from him nearly forty years ago. Lost. Surely dead. Yet there she stood in the lodge, beside the central fire. Its flame-light licked over her nut-brown skin, flashed in her nut-brown eyes, struck sparks in her curling, nut-brown hair. Others had called her looks odd, neither white, nor African, nor *Aniyunwiya*—The People, the *Tsalagi*—but a mix of all. Runs-Far thought her beautiful. He smiled to see her again, after all this time.

Walnut did not smile. With her neat little hands planted on narrow hips, she scowled as she used to when he had done a thing to vex her, back in the days when they were young, and a son and daughter played at their fire. Runs-Far's heart leapt to see that aggrieved expression, if only because it was clear time had dulled his memory of his young wife, leaving him with the rippled image one catches in water before a skin is dipped. This was Walnut's true self, sharp and clear.

Strange she should be scowling though. It was not the way a dead wife soon to reunite with a dying husband ought to look, over in that life-to-come where she had long been waiting with Creator-Jesus.

Unless Walnut was not waiting for him on the other side, but somewhere still on this side. Still living and waiting for him to find her.

"Those ones who chose your boy-name got it wrong, my husband," she said. "Runs-Far, they called you. Turns-Around-And-Goes-Home-Without-Trying is what they should have called you!"

"What?" The word croaked from his throat, long unused, even as dread built in Runs-Far's heart. "That is what you say to me, after these many years?"

"Did you expect better?" Walnut, always quick with her tongue, shot back. "Those soldiers took me from our village. But you did not come for me. You did not come for your child!"

The one unborn. Taken with its mother. It was true, though Runs-Far had managed not to think about it for a while, waiting for death to pounce. Now that old ache of guilt and grief took hold of his faltering heart.

"But I did. I came after you!"

Walnut waved a hand. "A little way only. Until the path split at your feet. Then you turned tail like a startled deer and bounded for home!"

Runs-Far remembered much about that terrible time he and Blue-Jay, their son, returned from their sojourn, taking word of Creator-Jesus to far-flung villages, to their people who had not yet heard. It was in a time of unrest, back when the British in the east had quarreled with the French in the west, with the Aniyunwiya caught in the middle, pressed to choose a side. Some had chosen the French and gone raiding eastern settlements. In retaliation, white men with rifles had come west over the mountains and raided Runs-Far's peaceful village, killing some.

Those soldiers had not killed his and Walnut's little daughter, Redwing, but had taken Walnut with her belly growing another child and carried her off, a prisoner. When Runs-Far and Blue-Jay returned much time had passed. The village had moved to new place. The soldiers' trail was cold.

Desperate with grief, he had traveled over many mountains to the place where that holy man who had taught him, Reverend Pauling, had not long since been buried, seeking help from those who had known and loved that good man, his hope no more than a thread. There that thread had snapped. That place had been deserted, the people gone from their houses, their fields abandoned. Gone to forts, as the white people did in times of war. A place he would find no welcome but be shot before he reached its gates.

There had been too many other places Walnut might have been taken by soldiers for him to know where next to search. The Carolinas. Georgia. Virginia. Or so he had believed. What path had he missed seeing?

"In your fear, you chose the wrong fork in that path," Walnut told him now. "It led you back the way you came, away from me. From our child. And not just us."

Distracted from paths by this mention of some other he had failed, Runs-Far tried to push himself up from his death-bed. The struggle left him panting, as he had done as a boy running up mountains. "Who else?"

"Him!" Walnut's chin tipped, pointing toward the lodge door.

As Runs-Far looked, the fire went out, plunging the lodge into blackness. No light showed at the door. He could see no one there. He could not see the hand he lifted before his face.

Death had sprung at last, he thought.

Then a Voice spoke, crooning through his soul with a mother's tenderness. Shaking his frame like thunder on a mountain.

"I know you, Timothy. By the Light that is in you and for My Name's sake you have continued your good work among your people and have not fainted. Yet I have this against you—your heart is on the ground where you left it long ago. You no longer love as you did. Remember where you left your heart. Take it off the ground and let it beat with the love it once knew. Else I will come again and next time I will remove your light from the earth."

Runs-Far lay trembling. He knew the Voice. And he understood that the place Walnut had spoken of, where the path had split, was the place he had left his heart lying on the ground. He was meant to return there.

But why did Creator send Walnut to tell him about splitting paths? Was he meant to seek for her again, as well as his own heart? How could he find a wife lost almost forty winters past? It was too much to expect of an old man. He had left it too late. And yet…the Voice had called to him when he had not heard even a whisper of it in so long. The Voice had called him *Timothy*.

"*Edo'da*!" he cried. Father.

And he woke.

Runs-Far opened his eyes and sat up, letting the blankets fall away. He was lying by the central fire in his snug, familiar lodge, which was not dark but bright with firelight. He saw its sturdy frames for storage and sleeping built against log walls hung with spare shirts and moccasins, with nets and frame-stretched hides, and his old bow with its quiver, dusty from disuse. He saw its earthen floor strewn with reed-mats woven by his daughter, and hers. And he saw the faces. Many faces ringing him. Startled faces enlivened by fire-shadows that leapt and bounced off chins and noses and blinking eyes.

These faces were not dreams, though some had aged since last he saw them, and it took a moment to put names to a few. His gaze settled last on one face he would know no matter where or when. The face of his eldest child.

Blue-Jay was no young man either, though grief had aged him beyond his fifty winters. Despite the beaded sheath-knife at his neck, the faded, blue-checked shirt he often wore, the leggings and breechclout that did not distinguish him from any other Tsalagi man present, he might have been a white man, this son born not of Runs-Far's body but of his prayers. Born with his father's skin and his mother's nut-brown eyes and hair, the latter streaked now with gray.

"Edo'da?" Blue-Jay said, first among the starers to speak. He had more chin hairs than did men born to the Aniyunwiya, another thing that marked his white blood. Though by habit he kept his face clean of them, it had been several days since he tended to that task. His cheeks were peppered with beard-stubble, his eyes bruised with care and little sleep.

Runs-Far's heart swelled with love, knowing himself the cause of both. Remembering he had been very ill. The grip of that illness had released him. He swallowed and rasped, "My son."

The words sent murmurs buzzing through the lodge, a sound like swarming bees. Blue-Jay's hand lifted, commanding silence. "Are you . . . ?" He stopped and made a second start. "We thought it time for you to . . . be going on."

Blue-Jay glanced to his right, where sat Thunder-Going-Away, chief of their village, hair hanging down from a blue head-wrapping like white wings to either side of his leathery face. Runs-Far smiled to see him. Then he remembered the Voice and what it had said.

"So I thought, too, that I would be going on to see the face of Creator at last. But that journey must wait. Creator has let me know that I have left a thing undone."

Blue-Jay gaped. "What have you left undone?"

Runs-Far saw beside him a horn cup. Taking it in trembling fingers he raised it and sipped. *Water.* He drank it down like courage for the thing he had next to tell his son, then set the cup aside.

"There is another journey I must make first."

The bee-hum erupted again. This time Blue-Jay did not silence it. His eyes had flown wide, making him appear much like the boy who still ran laughing through Runs-Far's memories. "Another journey?"

The true question stirred in his son's eyes. Was Runs-Far able to stand on his feet and walk across that lodge, much less make a journey?

"I am not dying today." Runs-Far pushed aside the blankets, bent stiffened legs, and gazed round at the staring faces. Clan, family, friends, those who had listened while year after year he taught of Creator-Jesus from the Holy Book the Reverend Pauling gave him long ago. "But neither am I getting younger. I need your help, my son."

"But Edo'da. Where is it you mean to go?"

It was a question Runs-Far could not answer. Not yet.

"I must find—" He tried to rise and fell back. It might be far, this journey he must take, but it would not be swift. He was wobbly as a spring fawn. Then he felt the arm of his son around him, strong and sure, and changed what he meant to say. One word of it. "*We* must find your mother."

1

Anuyi — Windy Moon to *Kawani* — Flower Moon (March — April)

THUNDER-GOING-AWAY'S TOWN

"Stop thwarting our father and help him make this journey!"

Redwing's sharp tone, a rare sound from his younger sister, made Blue-Jay straighten from her fire, which he had been poking with a stick. Redwing had been sorting through baskets on the other side of her lodge but faced him now. Firelight glinted off the silver ring-brooches pinned around the neck of her red-dyed dress, which fell to the knees of her blue tradecloth leggings—and it flashed in her eyes as she glanced at three of her grandchildren sitting across the fire, staring at their uncle like a row of round-eyed owlets.

Blue-Jay swallowed back the words he had intended to add to the explanation he had been making—not for the first time—as to why traipsing over mountains with their father in hopes of discovering what happened to their long-lost mother was a bad idea.

Though it was near the end of the Bone Moon when Runs-Far opened his eyes and declared it was not his day to die, it had taken more days for him to regain strength enough even to leave his lodge. Many had passed since then. The snows were receding up the mountains now. During all that time, Runs-Far had been readying himself to set out on the journey neither Blue-Jay nor anyone else could dissuade him from making.

One person had refrained even from trying to dissuade—Redwing. Now, after days of listening to Blue-Jay recount the arguments that had fallen on their father's deaf ears, his sister stared hard at him, heaved a sigh, then herded her grandchildren out of her lodge. When they were alone, she turned with hands on hips to face Blue-Jay. He stared back at her, a little offended, pained that she did not seem to understand the matter. Could she not see that their father was still frail, that death could come for him again? Did she want that happening far away, as it must have done for their mother?

Something in his expression—he would never know what—made his sister's soften with compassion. "Brother, listen to me. It is as much for *you* and your grief, your need, as it is for our father and his, that you must make this journey."

Blue-Jay opened his mouth, then shut it, having no idea what to say to that. She had not mentioned Blue-Jay's second wife, taken from him in the bleak cold days when that fever ravaged the town—the same they had thought would take their father. Still a stone lodged in Blue-Jay's throat. "It is senseless to think we will learn anything of our mother after all this time."

"Probably." Redwing came to the fire to sit beside him. Against his shoulder she leaned her head, crowned in hair as black as their father's had once been, though a few white hairs threaded hers now. Though her face was wide at the cheekbones and brow, also like their father, she had the shape of their mother's lips and her small but stubborn chin. "Still the journey may prove a good thing. For both of you."

"It is more likely to kill him. What if—"

Redwing's head jerked upright. Her dark eyes drilled into him. "While you have argued with our father's choice, I have made my peace with it. If he never returns, *you* will—to tell me of his passing and where he is buried, and whether you each found what you sought. This you must promise to do."

Though Blue-Jay had more of their mother's looks—the nut-brown hair and eyes, the length of his nose, the set of his jaw, even the shape of his ears—in her soul his sister was most like the woman called Walnut. Redwing's mind and heart were steady. She knew when she was right about a thing.

He pretended not to understand. "What do *I* seek?"

"Healing." Redwing flattened her mouth when he frowned. "I am not talking about the grief of this winter. I do not even mean the hurt of the daughter who died all those years ago, that spring the river flooded. I mean the hurt you have carried longest, since our mother was taken. You know what that is. I do not need to name it. If you do not find a way to heal it on this journey with our father, you never will. This is Creator's doing. His gift. You had better accept it and go."

Blue-Jay raised his hands. "Go where? I do not know which path to take."

Redwing's smile was soft, a little sad. "That is for Creator to show our father, in His time. Have a little faith."

"Just a little?" Blue-Jay muttered but had no more argument to make with his sister's counsel. A little faith—a mere seed—that was all he could claim.

Too little, he feared.

UPPER YADKIN RIVER VALLEY, NORTH CAROLINA

The Windy Moon—the time the whites called *March*—was waning when Blue-Jay and Runs-Far bid farewell to their relations. Most who had gathered for the death that had not happened had returned to their homes. Two had stayed, both friends of the Aniyunwiya. Each had been adopted long ago by a certain warrior of the Shawnees, the people who dwelled to the north, across the great river, to be his brothers. One was born white. Panther-Sees-Him was the name the Shawnees gave that one. He now lived in the part of the whites' territory called Kentucky with his white wife and children, where he was known as Jeremiah Ring.

The other was born of a Lenape mother, enslaved on a Virginia plantation, before he became the Shawnee warrior called Wolf-Alone. These days he went by the name of Cade. That one was an old friend of Thunder-Going-Away, peace chief of Blue-Jay and Runs-Far's town.

Cade and Jeremiah Ring had lingered through the Windy Moon, waiting for Runs-Far to be ready to start the journey, which would begin at a place not far from Cade's home.

"MacKinnon's Cove, North Carolina," Runs-Far had announced. "That is where it starts." He would not say why, though Blue-Jay thought it must have to do with the Reverend Pauling. What that could be, seeing as that man died before their mother was even taken, he could not say. But it was the reason Cade and Jeremiah Ring had waited. The two had planned to journey together for a time anyway before each was needed to help with the planting of crops on their respective farms, so they were content to do this thing.

Blue-Jay was grateful. Though he had roamed the mountains of his people all his life, much of that land was now under the governing of the new state, Tennessee. Many whites had come pouring over the mountains to live there. Blue-Jay looked white—to be reminded of it always surprised—but they were not his people, and he had never been to MacKinnon's Cove.

"The MacKinnons are neighbors," Cade said when the name first fell from Runs-Far's lips. Though he was half white and had lived among them, Cade's skin was nearly as dark, his hair still mostly as black, as many of the Tsalagi. He wore a brown felted hat like a white man's with a hawk's feather thrust through the brim. "We—my nephew, his wife, and I—settled near the MacKinnons ten years back. It's but a few days' journey from here."

They took longer than a few days to cover the distance. Runs-Far had not regained his former strength and he, like Blue-Jay, Cade, and Jeremiah Ring, carried his provisions and all he would need in a wide square bag with a woven strap slung across his chest, a trade-wool blanket folded over one shoulder. The rest also carried shot-bags and powder horns for the rifles they toted in their hands. Runs-Far carried a walking stick instead of a gun. It was also still the time of thawing in the high country, the trails thick with mud in places to slow them down. They wore gaiters tied or buttoned to their knees to keep their leggings clean. Each carried spare moccasins in his bag, and the tools to repair them.

Blue-Jay's father had spoken little during the first days of their journey, needing his breath for climbing mountains during the day, eager for his blanket whenever they camped. Blue-Jay held his peace and did not question his father about what he hoped to find at MacKinnon's Cove. Perhaps it would be nothing, and they could end this journey almost before it had begun.

It was a happy thought Blue-Jay did not wish dispelled.

The Flower Moon had come before they arrived at the homestead Cade and his nephew had built in a high cleft between mountain slopes forested in conifers and leafing hardwoods. Through it tumbled one of the Yadkin's many feeder creeks. A tall, white-washed house, strangely looming to Blue-Jay's eyes, accustomed to smaller cabins and earth-dug winter lodges, overlooked slanting fields ready for plowing, and a small apple orchard in bloom. Tucked up along one ridgeline near the house was a large structure that smelled of animals, others that Blue-Jay took in without identifying.

As they filed out of the forest past a scrim of dogwood still bearing its white mantle, a dog that appeared at least half wolf sprang up from where it had been dozing, outside the place that smelled of animals, and eyed them. It flattened it ears and, with a noise more howl than bark, loped across the yard to halt in front of Cade, where it rose to its hind legs and twisted its lanky self in an alarming dance of welcome.

Cade thumped his rifle butt on the ground and slapped his broad chest. Though he was a tall man, that dog stood and planted its paws on Cade's broad shoulders, letting the man fondle its shaggy head, mouth agape to show rows of sharp white teeth. When he thrust the dog aside, it greeted Jeremiah Ring, though without the paws on the shoulders.

Blue-Jay and Runs-Far hung back, but the dog was having none of their shyness. It came next to greet them. Jeremiah grinned through the dark beginnings of a beard gone unshaved while they traveled. "Let him get your scent."

Blue-Jay proffered his hand for the animal to sniff, though he clenched his rifle with the other. Runs-Far held tight to his walking stick, leaning on it. At the end of their sixth day of travel he was clearly too tired to be worried about wolf-dogs. Even his eyes, set at a slight up-tilt at their outer corners, drooped like the lined brown skin that sagged along his once-firm jaw.

His father seemed shrunken, smaller than the man he had been before the sickness, his broad cheekbones too sharply defined.

"See?" Jeremiah Ring said. "He won't jump up uninvited."

"We've managed to teach him a few manners," someone coming across the yard called. Tongue lolling, the dog loped back to the speaker, a white man younger than any in their party, with sun-streaked brown hair tailed back from a hawkish face.

He gave them greeting in the language of The People. "*Osiyo. Detsayadanilvga. Osigwotsu*?"

Blue-Jay answered for himself and his father. "*Osda*... we are well. *S'gi*." Thank you.

"Jesse Kincaid, my nephew," Cade introduced as the younger man reached them. He named Blue-Jay and Runs-Far. "The dog ain't been with us long."

Jesse knuckled the animal's head. "Came out of the woods last autumn, after the first snow. Ribs showing and an arrow in his haunch. Wouldn't let us near him. We put up the chickens, set out some scraps. Day or two of that, he let us take the arrow out."

"And before we knew it," a female voice added, "he was sleeping at our hearth. I call him Dargo, because darned if he'll go."

A woman in a faded skirt that might once have been the color of raspberries, its front covered in a plain linen garment Blue-Jay thought called an *apron*, had stepped from the house. Pretty as a dark-eyed flower, she stood on a raised platform built along the front of the house, smiling in welcome, not at all startled by strangers in her yard, Indian or otherwise. The apron she wore poked out in front in a way that made it clear she was with child. Blue-Jay noted this as four more children came bursting out of the house behind her and clattered down the porch steps, dressed like their parents in miniature, their feet in moccasins.

"Uncle Cade!" they cried, save the eldest, a boy of about nine summers. He seemed as happy as the rest to see their kinsman returned but was, Blue-Jay guessed, trying to be grown up about it.

Jesse made introductions, starting with the woman standing above them, his wife, who told them to call her Tamsen. The quiet, dark-haired boy who stared with open interest at Blue-Jay and Runs-Far was called Bryan. Next was a girl with braided hair colored like her father's, undecided between brown and blond. "Just shy of eight, our Sarah. And a fine help to her mama."

Sarah's cheeks pinked as she made a little bob like a bird dipping in a stream.

"There's Stephen, he's six. And wee Fiona is four." Jessie patted the head of the youngest, a dark-eyed miniature of her mother, whose hair was nearly black.

Fiona bobbed in imitation of her sister, then raced back to the house to duck behind her mother's skirt. Blue-Jay followed the child with his gaze, a small catch in his chest. That one hiding behind her mother might have been his own little daughter. At least how he remembered her.

"Weren't expecting you back for another fortnight." Jesse shot a glance at Blue-Jay and Runs-Far. "Did the passel of you go to Long Meadows?"

"How is Cousin Ambrose?" Tamsen asked as they mounted steps made of wood planks to join her. She gave Jeremiah Ring a murmured greeting before Cade spoke.

"We ain't made it to Long Meadows yet. Meaning still to go—shorter visit than planned."

"Something happen at Thunder-Going-Away's Town?" Jesse's gaze sharpened. "Wait… Runs-Far. Ain't that the one you went to…?"

"I am that one." Blue-Jay's father managed a smile though weariness cloaked him like mist on the mountains. "I did not pass on as everyone thought I meant to do. As you see."

Jesse's brows vaulted. "I do see. But what brings you so far from home?"

Cade nodded at Blue-Jay and his father. "These two are bound for MacKinnon's Cove. But that'll wait for tomorrow. Explanations can bide, too."

Tamsen's gaze rested on Runs-Far, holding to Blue-Jay's arm after climbing the steps. "Strip off those gaiters and come in, all of you. We'll share supper, then you can rest the night."

Cade, who had already unfastened his muddy gaiters, opened the door, through which the children passed, all talking at once. Blue-Jay helped his father, too stiff to bend, to shed his.

Tamsen let the others file into her home as Jesse took her aside. "I've that scythe blade I been meaning to take to MacKinnon's smithy for repair. I'll go along tomorrow if you'll be all right. Be back afore suppertime."

Tamsen rested a hand across the child in her belly, which did not look many more weeks from being born. Last to pass into the strange house where boards creaked under moccasins and steps led up to more house built on top of the rooms below, Blue-Jay caught more of the conversation on the other side of the open door.

"I'll be fine, Jesse."

"You sure? Just this mornin' you felt unwell."

"Not unwell, exactly. Something's just different with this one . . ."

Inside the house a child's laughter spiraled high. Blue-Jay missed whatever else the two coming in behind him might have said.

The children were being put into their beds. Blue-Jay, Cade, and Jeremiah Ring sat outside the house—on the *porch*, they called it—in chairs brought outside, smoking pipes while twilight crept up the narrow valley that was, Cade had told Blue-Jay, separated from MacKinnon's Cove by a couple of ridges rising to the east. Runs-Far slept on a pallet spread on the floor of the front room.

Blue-Jay felt the tiredness of mountain-walking in his bones. Soon he would join his father. For the moment he was content to sit with these men and watch the eastern hills purple with the dusk.

After a bit, Jesse came outside and settled on the steps, his lanky wolf-dog beside him. "Tamsen's tired," he told the men arrayed across the porch in chairs. "She bids y'all good-night. I'll cook us up some vittles in the morning. Then we'll be on our way to MacKinnon's."

Blue-Jay heard worry in the younger man's tone. Apparently so did Cade. "You troubled, Jesse?"

"Wish we'd a midwife over at MacKinnon's still. Least one with more experience."

"What happened to the one tended your other young'uns?" Jeremiah asked.

"She was elderly. Passed on a month back, sudden-like."

"What about Tamsen coming with us?" Cade asked. "To Long Meadows. There's sure to be a choice of midwives within hail of your cousin Ambrose's plantation. A physician or two, come to that."

A sigh rose from the young man perched on the steps, fingers buried in the dog's ruff. "I brought it up a week back. Tamsen don't fancy making the journey to Lynchburg. Unless she has to."

Cade gave a nod. "Don't take long deciding. I'd hightail it back here, mind things, should Tamsen change her mind."

Jesse's nod was just visible in the falling dark.

Blue-Jay knew well the worry the young man harbored. His own first wife had died trying to bring a son into the world, so long ago he could not recall her face. He hoped Jesse Kincaid would not lose his pretty, dark-eyed wife with this birth. Under his breath he whispered to Creator about it.

Jeremiah knocked the dottle from his pipe over the porch rail, done with smoking. Cade and Blue-Jay followed suit. The dog rose and leapt off the steps, loping out into the dark.

Blue-Jay cleared his throat. Addressing Cade, he said, "This Long Meadows you speak of, is that not the plantation where you were born a slave? Yet you mean to go back to it?"

"I've been back a time or two already, to visit my father before he passed—and my nephew, Ambrose Kincaid, master there now."

Blue-Jay supposed much history lay behind those words, spoken by a man who had lived at least three lives: born a slave, adopted a Shawnee, now living free in the mountains of North Carolina with his white nephew.

"How are you no longer a slave?"

Cade obliged him with the bare bones of his story. "My father was master of Long Meadows when I was born to one of his Lenape slaves. He'd two white sons who knew me for their half-brother. One was kind, the other cruel. When the kind one married and left Virginia to settle here, he took me with him. As a brother, not a slave. Jesse was born. Life was good. Then—and this bit I've pieced together since—while I was off hunting our brother showed up. I'll never know exactly what fell out between them all, but he killed Jesse's parents while Jesse, hardly more'n a baby, hid in the barn. Shawnee hunters found the cabin burning, and Jesse, still hiding out. I come home to find my family dead, Jesse gone, and a trail of prints heading north. I buried my kin then followed that trail, not knowing where it would lead."

Jesse took up the story. "Those Shawnees took me over the Ohio River. I was adopted and called Wildcat. Cade found me, but enough time had passed I'd forgotten him. After I grew up a bit, he became like an uncle to me—as the warrior, Wolf-Alone—before I knew he *was* my uncle."

Cade's voice warmed as he glanced at Blue-Jay. "You already know I got myself adopted by a warrior of that same village—who already had this one for a brother." He gave the arm of Jeremiah Ring, seated beside him, an amiable punch. "After Virginia's governor made war with the Shawnees and Wildcat's adopted father was killed, we struck out on our own, Jesse and me. Changed our names. Eventually settled over in the Watauga country."

"That's when Tamsen came into our story," Jesse said, a grin in his voice. "And my cousin, Ambrose."

"He is the son of that other brother?" Blue-Jay asked. "The cruel one who did the killing?"

Cade nodded. "Ambrose, he's a different cast. Not like his father. When we came back to this place at last, he was here waiting to greet us. So was my father. I could never be what he was, an owner of other men, but I made my peace with him before his death."

"A few years back," Jeremiah said, "Cade and I crossed paths again over to Cumberland Gap, each thinking the other gone to Glory, mighty happy to discover otherwise. Since I've never seen Long Meadows, we're headed that way for a visit."

"We'll stay a few days with Ambrose," Cade said, "then head back this way."

"Then I'll head back over the Gap to Clare, my wife," Jeremiah said. "Though these days, Jacob, our eldest, does the lion's share of the farming. He's raising up his own brood on our homeplace. Our eldest daughter lives with her husband over near Boonesborough. The rest are soon to fly the nest, I reckon."

It was good to listen to these men talk of their children—even Cade, who had no offspring to speak of but did have his nephew, a connection closer for many men than their own children. Blue-Jay considered speaking of Redwing's children, who he had loved and nurtured as an uncle should, but Jesse put a question to him that sent the talk down another trail.

"What business takes you and your pa over to MacKinnons'? If you don't mind my asking."

Blue-Jay did not mind, but he was not the one with the answer. That one lay sleeping, guarding his full purpose—or perhaps the fact that he did not have one.

"We are trying to learn what happened to my mother, lost many years ago, back when there was trouble between the Tsalagi and the British."

"The old French War?" Jesse asked. "And by *lost* do you mean captured?"

"Yes, to both." Blue-Jay hesitated, then decided to say more. "My mother had the blood of the Tsalagi in her veins—other blood, some white. She was born a plantation slave on a river called Cape Fear, where the man who fathered me lived. She escaped that place with me in her belly. My true father, Runs-Far, was a very young man when the war party he was with found my mother. She was trying to birth me, but I was not coming forth. My father put his hands on my mother's belly and prayed to Creator, in the name of Jesus, and out I came. My mother was adopted by an old aunt she found among the Tsalagi. My father took her as wife, me as his son. My sister was born. Another child was coming when soldiers raided our village and took my mother. My father was away on one of his journeys, telling the people in other villages of Creator-Jesus, and I . . . I was with him. The only time I ever went. I had marked twelve summers."

Jeremiah and Cade had heard the story. It was new to Jesse, who had swiveled on the porch steps to face Blue-Jay, his hawk's face bathed in faint firelight from inside the house. "Didn't your pa go looking afore now?"

"We were long returning from our journey. The trail was cold. My father went to MacKinnon's Cove. Other than that, I do not know where he looked."

"Why MacKinnon's Cove?"

"It must have to do with Reverend Pauling."

"Who?"

"We never met the man, Jesse," Cade said. "He died long before we knew the Cherokees, or the MacKinnons. Thunder-Going-Away knew the reverend when he was young."

"Pauling," Jesse said after a moment's thought. "He was that missionary?"

Blue-Jay nodded. "My father was first of our town—it was Crooked Branch's Town then—to believe the teachings. Runs-Far taught the ways of Creator-Jesus long after the reverend grew too old to cross the mountains. I was young still, the last time he came. He is buried at MacKinnon's Cove, my father tells me."

"How's visiting his grave meant to help you find what happened to your mother?"

"Not his grave, but maybe those who knew him." Having no better answer to give Jesse made Blue-Jay feel foolish now to be sitting on this porch in the dark, having come so far with his father, chasing after ghosts. Loneliness engulfed him as the silence stretched. His heart weighed heavy with loss—including the one he had evaded for now; his father's death, which would come maybe sooner than later, far from home, among strangers with no understanding of the journey they had made.

Cade broke the silence. "I think, Jesse, this is one of those journeys a man must make not knowing where he's going, or if he'll find what he seeks at its end. Like when you were taken by the Shawnees and I came after you—and found myself some brothers besides," he added, with a glance at Jeremiah.

"Yes." Blue-Jay nearly choked on the word. These men, at least, understood. "It is a journey like that."

But what unexpected thing would he and his father find at its end? Something good, as Cade had found, or only more loss?

2

Kawoni — Flower Moon (April)

MACKINNON'S COVE, NORTH CAROLINA

MacKinnon's Cove resembled Cade and Jesse's homestead, if one were to double the main dwelling then repeat it in varying sizes, with attending barns and fields and orchards, down the length of a broadening mountain cove to a distant river, glinting as it curved away eastward through lower hills.

"That river yonder's the Yadkin," Cade said as the trail they followed emerged from forest pink-laced with redbud blooms and emptied onto the mossy bank of a chattering creek, spanned by a log footbridge. Beyond the creek, across a sloping patch of grass, stood another tall white house. This one's porch was deep and wrapped it front and sides. From the house a track descended, winding its way past the dwellings and fields below.

Upslope behind the house, where the mountain rose too steep for planting, the creek issued from the forest in a short but forceful fall over a stony ledge. There something Blue-Jay recognized, a small mill, had been constructed. Many years ago to judge by the weathered timbers.

"A grist mill," Jesse told them. "Built by the cove's namesake. Alex MacKinnon."

Blue-Jay and his father exchanged a look. Runs-Far had known Alex MacKinnon, once very well. An indentured man fleeing an injustice done him at the place Blue-Jay's mother—then called Jemma—was enslaved, Alex MacKinnon had brought her away with him, heading west until their path crossed that of the Aniyunwiya. Because of this, Blue-Jay had become the son of Runs-Far.

It was many years since Alex MacKinnon had come into their country. Not since before Blue-Jay's mother was taken and they abandoned Crooked Branch's Town and found another place to live, far to the westward. Blue-Jay had assumed the man was dead, but now he thought about it... maybe not. How old would he be? Not yet eighty winters, though not far off that mark. Could Alex MacKinnon help them learn what happened to Blue-Jay's mother, after she was carried off?

Anticipation gripped his father's face as they crossed the footbridge into the yard of the house. Runs-Far had not asked Cade or Jesse whether Alex MacKinnon lived. The name had not once passed his father's lips. Blue-Jay could guess why. Hope endured in not knowing.

Downstream of the footbridge, under an old chestnut, stood the shop of the blacksmith Jesse had come to visit. The sun was barely risen but already a rhythmic *clink* issued from the structure. A horse stood hitched in the chestnut's broad shade.

Blue-Jay smelled food cooking.

Cade led them up to the house with its porch, in the shade of which two rocking chairs stood empty. Blue-Jay could imagine two old people, a man and woman, sitting in them at the end of a day, looking down over that cove.

They had reached the foot of the steps leading up to the door when a piercing squeal halted them. Around the house's nearest corner a pair of children came tearing—a small girl with coppery braids flying, on her heels a smaller red-haired boy wearing nothing but a clout. They galloped barefoot over spring grass, darting furtive backward glances.

Charging around the house with a panther's screech, arms outstretched and fingers clawed in pursuit, came a young woman with freckled skin and hair curling like flames from under a white cap.

"I'm a'coming for ye, ring-tailed rascals. I'm—"

Catching sight of them, the woman staggered to a halt. The girl ran smack into Blue-Jay. The boy sprawled at his feet. Too surprised at finding strangers in his yard to cry over the tumble, he stared up at Blue-Jay with hazel eyes gone round as pebbles. Dirt smeared his cheek and his little round belly.

Barefoot as the little ones she chased, with green stains on the apron covering the front of a skirt sprinkled with blue flowers, the young woman recovered herself with a laugh.

"Jesse and Cade! Ain't ye heard of hallooing a house when ye come calling? Ye here for the smithy?" she asked before either could answer the first question, nodding at the scythe blade peeking from the sacking Jesse had wrapped it in. She had a chin that ended in a point, as did her freckled nose.

Jesse grinned at the woman. "For a fact, Sally MacKinnon. The rest got other business. Who's to home this morning?"

"Not Papa Edmund. He's gone down the cove to see a man about a cow. Let me think..." Sally ticked off names on her fingers. "My Micah's turning up a field for planting. Papa 'Lijah's in the schoolroom waiting on the young'uns to come up the cove. Granny Jo's about someplace—kitchen garden, last I saw, with Mama Zilpha. Ye've run smack into Marigold and Abel." She scooped the boy off the ground, brushed off his clouted bottom, and gave Jeremiah Ring, Blue-Jay, and Runs-Far a nod. The hammering, which had paused, struck up again. "As ye hear, Uncle Jory's got the forge fired up. I 'spect he's time to work ye in, Jesse, this early in the day."

"Go see to it," Cade told his nephew. "We'll find Mrs. MacKinnon."

"*I*'m Mrs. MacKinnon," Sally said as Jesse struck off toward the smithy. "One of 'em, anyway. But I'm guessing it ain't me ye come to see. Be it Mama Zilpha or Granny Jo ye're looking for?"

"Joanna MacKinnon," Runs-Far said, surprising Blue-Jay, who thought that was the name of Alex MacKinnon's wife. Was this the one Sally had called Granny Jo? The anticipation on his father's face was now almost painful to see, as his big-knuckled fingers gripped his walking stick. Even Blue-Jay's heart was banging.

"If she's feeling up to a visit," Cade added.

"Granny Jo?" Sally laughed. "Seventy she be. Still running circles round me most days. Marigold," she said to the little girl dressed in a garment made of the same cloth as her mother's skirt. "Run find your great-granny. Tell her she's guests a'waiting inside."

"Yes, Mama." The girl bounded back around the house, little bare heels flashing.

Sally waited for them to shed bags and rifles on the porch. Once inside, she set the boy on his feet to toddle ahead into the room into which she led them. It was the second white dwelling Blue-Jay had entered in the past two days. This one was older, more established, than that of their neighbors across the ridge. The rugs on the plank floors and the treads of a wide stairway near the front of the house showed the wear of many feet, but the furnishings of the room into which they stepped were of a higher quality—to Blue-Jay's untrained eye. More striking were its walls, painted a yellowish gold. It was like walking into the sun.

There were many places to sit, but their gazes followed the toddling boy through a doorway into another, plainer room, where an old man's voice welcomed him, though the speaker was not in their line of view.

"That's the schoolroom yonder," Sally said, then lifted her voice to call, "Papa 'Lijah? We've company here. Ye might want to greet 'em afore your students arrive."

There came a shuffling of steps. A moment later, holding to the little boy's lifted hand, a man emerged from the room beyond that yellow one. He had hair white as sun-on-snow, tailed back from a face wrinkled and age-spotted, and badly scarred down its right side. He was not a tall man but must have once been powerfully built. Even now his shoulders filled out his linen shirt, over which he wore a sleeveless vest that buttoned over his thickened middle. Blue eyes shone bright in the ravaged face, regarding Cade with recognition, the rest with a keen curiosity.

Blue-Jay's gaze dropped to the man's right arm, to which the boy was attached. It was not a hand to which the child clung, but a knotted shirtsleeve where a hand was missing.

"This is Papa 'Lijah—Elijah Moon—my husband Micah's granddaddy, on his mama's side," Sally said by way of introduction.

Elijah Moon gave his great-grandson a pat on the bottom to shoo him back to Sally. He gave Cade a neighborly nod. "I be what passes for a schoolmaster in these parts. Long back I was blacksmith. Before this." He raised the stump of a wrist. "'Tis my eldest son, Jory, and his son, Eliot, seeing to that business now."

The man had the speech of some type of the English, born across the great water. Not a high-born type, Blue-Jay did not think.

Cade introduced Jeremiah Ring, Blue-Jay, and Runs-Far, at whose name a light sprang into Elijah Moon's eyes. "Runs-Far be a name I recall..."

Before he could say more, other voices rose. Women had entered the house from somewhere down the central passage. From the schoolroom, where there must have been another door to the yard, came the rambunctious calls of older children entering the house.

"Mean ye to bide the day?" Elijah Moon asked, already pivoting toward the schoolroom. "I be teaching 'til dinner."

Cade assured the old man they would stay for dinner if it was no trouble. Elijah Moon nodded and went to greet his students, closing that door as two women entered the room.

Both were gowned in printed skirts not unlike the one Sally wore, but otherwise much different in age and appearance. One was as white-haired as old Elijah Moon, shrunken with age but spry enough to walk without much stiffness in her bearing. The other was taller, with a handsome face a light golden brown, showing the lines of middle years. The dark hair not pinned up high on her head hung long and coiled. Her eyes were as blue as Elijah Moon's, striking in her honeyed face.

"Here they be." Sally touched the arm of the younger of the two. "This is Mama Zilpha. She and Papa Edmund—the one down the cove just now—are my Micah's parents. She's also Papa 'Lijah and Granny Marigold's eldest daughter. Granny Mari—God rest her—is who my Marigold is called after. And if that ain't enough names yet to spin your heads," she added with a sweeping grin at Blue-Jay, Runs-Far, and Jeremiah Ring, "I can give ye more. We're a proper clan here on the mountain, cousins of one stripe or another, with a few like me married in for spice."

The woman called Zilpha, with the blue eyes and honeyed skin, smiled at her son's wife, but the older woman had stopped short at sight of Runs-Far and Blue-Jay. She was still staring at them when Sally said, "And this here be the one ye say ye've come to see—"

"Joanna MacKinnon." Runs-Far stepped toward the white-haired woman, whose puzzled gaze shifted from Blue-Jay's father to Blue-Jay himself. When at last she spoke, voice quavering with age, Blue-Jay felt the shock of her words in his bones and pounding heart.

"You're Jemma's son. You must be. I see her looking at me with your eyes."

With the door to the schoolroom closed on the voices within, Zilpha, daughter of Elijah Moon and wife of Edmund MacKinnon, Joanna's eldest son—if Blue-Jay had grasped these kinship connections—had taken hold of the older woman's arm and led her to a chair made comfortable with cushions. The rest took other seats. Sally had gone to the kitchen out behind the house and fetched a tray with tea and a plate of a sweetened bread cut into squares, smelling of strange spices.

Cade and Jeremiah Ring sipped from their cups while they talked about the doings of that place and its people. With his father perched beside him on the edge of a padded bench, Blue-Jay was too tense to take in the half of it.

Joanna MacKinnon had barely taken her gaze from them. Finally she cut into the talk of small matters. "Is it true? You're Jemma's son? And you…" Her gaze shifted to Runs-Far. "Her husband?"

Blue-Jay felt their otherness like a screaming in that room. They were dressed in moccasins, their fringed shirts belted with tomahawk and knife, like Cade and Jeremiah Ring, but where those two had changed that morning into the knee breeches of white men, Blue-Jay and his father still wore their leggings and breechclouts.

"I am that one," Blue-Jay's father said. "I am Runs-Far. Also called Timothy, by one you knew. Reverend Pauling."

"Yes." The word was spoken breathlessly as Joanna MacKinnon bent forward. "And Jemma?"

"That is what my wife was called before she became Sedi—*Walnut*, you would say."

"Walnut is the one Alex MacKinnon brought across my father's path," Blue-Jay added, "the day I was being born."

Runs-Far had not broken Joanna MacKinnon's steady gaze. "But that much I think you know."

The old woman nodded her head, upon which hair thick for her years was swept into a braided knot, not covered by a cap as the younger women wore. "I was there the day she was born, at Severn Plantation. Jemma—Jemima—we called her. She was enslaved to my stepfather until she ran away with Alex, that time he left us." The woman's lips parted in a smile that revealed old teeth still in their places. "*Stole herself*, I'm sure she would have said."

Blue-Jay felt a tug at his own mouth, remembering the few times his mother had talked of that life before she came to the Tsalagi. "She did say things like that."

Thoughts unreadable stirred in Joanna MacKinnon's eyes. "I cannot get over how strikingly you resemble her, aside from your complexion. Not at all like . . ."

She faltered, leaving Blue-Jay to wonder what she had started to say. Had she nearly spoken of the man his mother ran from? The man he had always suspected was the one who had fathered him. A man his parents had never named. Not in Blue-Jay's presence.

Zilpha turned to her husband's mother. "Didn't Papa Alex say, last time he went to the Cherokees, he found their town abandoned? You've wondered ever since what became of them."

"We wondered many things." Joanna's eyes were a color that shifted with the window's light, grayish green in full sunlight, browner when a cloud passed over. "But Jemma. Isn't she with you?"

"We hoped she came before us," Runs-Far said.

"Before you?" Zilpha's gaze darted around the room as if Blue-Jay's mother might be hiding behind a chair.

"Has she up and run away *again*?" Sally asked.

Runs-Far drew himself straight. "I will tell you the part of her story which you do not yet know, if you would hear it."

"I very much wish to hear it," Joanna said.

Cade, quiet until now, said, "First, Jeremiah and I best head down to the smithy. Jesse's going back to Tamsen today, but we're bound for Virginia from here. You'll be all right?" he asked Blue-Jay.

At his nod, Cade and Jeremiah left the women staring expectantly at Runs-Far, who told the last story they knew of Walnut, once called Jemma, ending with Runs-Far coming to MacKinnon's Cove, seeking help in finding her. "No one was here. All the places stood empty. I found only graves. Reverend Pauling's among them."

Joanna was frowning, as if trying to recall the long-ago time of which Runs-Far had spoken. "If that was during the French War, we would have fled to the forts for safety."

Runs-Far nodded. "It is what I thought."

Sally gazed from Runs-Far to Blue-Jay. "That all the hunting ye did? Coming here?"

"No other places to look." Blue-Jay swept a hand toward the window that gave view of the cove. "Or too many. All the places."

Joanna understood. "She might have been taken anywhere."

"With no trail to follow, my father could do no more." As Blue-Jay spoke, his father's face grew shuttered. Then he remembered his father saying he had left a thing undone. Runs-Far did not believe what Blue-Jay had just said in his defense was true. It was why they had come.

"I'm just aggrieved we weren't here when you needed us." Joanna leaned forward again. "I owe you so much, you see. All that I have. My very life."

Sally's wasn't the only breath drawn at the declaration. Runs-Far alone showed no surprise. "The buffalo."

Joanna sat back in her chair, eyes shining in wrinkled beds. "Yes. That buffalo."

"Buffalo?" Sally asked. "I ain't heard tell of buffalo in these mountains for years."

"'Twas a different world," Joanna said. "Half a century ago." To Runs-Far she added, "You were with him, of course. With Alex. Would you care to tell it?"

Runs-Far was smiling now. "I will tell it. It is a good tale."

It was one Blue-Jay had heard, a thing that happened while he was a baby in Walnut's arms. How Alex MacKinnon joined the hunters of Crooked Branch's Town, including Runs-Far, to bring down mountain buffalo to feed the people. They had found a small herd. Hunters had stampeded it through a draw where they could be shot. One buffalo had charged at Runs-Far, who had never hunted the creatures before that day. Neither had Alex MacKinnon, but seeing Runs-Far about to be trampled, he had called out to the God of Reverend Pauling for help, then shot an arrow at the beast, which turned at the last moment and had not trampled Runs-Far to death. "He thought the arrow flew wild. Still the buffalo swerved. Creator spared my life that day. How was yours saved by it?"

Joanna's smile deepened the crinkles at her eyes. "That was the moment Alex surrendered himself to the Almighty. It was the start of his journey back to me, which he made in time to save me and others from...a man intent on harming us," she finished with another glance at Blue-Jay, who felt a sickly knot form in his belly.

Was the man Alex MacKinnon saved her from the same that had made his mother flee that place on the Cape Fear River? The one she never named.

"It was a few more years before we lost touch with those we knew at Crooked Branch's Town," Joanna was telling his father. "Including you and Jemma. Reverend Pauling carried our messages until he grew too ill to do so. His last months were spent with us, which is why he's buried on our mountain."

Runs-Far nodded. "I know Reverend Pauling was put into the ground here. I saw that place, that time before. I wish for your permission to walk upon that ground again. But first I would see Alex MacKinnon. Is he away with your son, Edmund, or down there working in the smithy?"

"Papa Alex stopped working the smithy ages ago," Zilpha replied. "My brother, Jory, is blacksmith now. He's training up his son, Eliot."

"Where then is Alex MacKinnon?" Runs-Far asked. "I much desire to see him again."

Joanna and Zilpha exchanged a look, then the younger woman stood to help the other to rise. Blue-Jay and his father stood too, the tea in their cups grown cold.

"He's nearby," Joanna said, beckoning them from the room. "I'll take you to him."

3

Joanna MacKinnon did not lead them to another room, where a man might be lying abed, too old or too ill to come out to them. She led them straight through the house and out its back.

Asking no questions, Blue-Jay and Runs-Far followed at her pace down beaten paths between gardens, Blue-Jay deciding Alex MacKinnon must still be strong enough to be working somewhere beyond the house and yard. He remembered him as a big man—once a warrior in his native Scotland, taller than any man in the village, strong and fierce. Such a one might well retain his vigor long past the age most men diminished.

Leaving behind the outbuildings clustered near the house, the path ran toward the grist-mill with its waterfall, its grinding stones silent. Joanna did not head for the mill. When the path branched away from it and the water's noise lessened, she paused to speak.

"Our youngest, Samuel, tends the mill now. Today he's working his fields, down the cove where he lives."

Runs-Far indicated the silent structure. "Is that not where we are going?"

Joanna shook her head and motioned to the path. "This way."

Was Alex MacKinnon still working the ground? The path angled up a wooded rise that left Joanna clinging to Blue-Jay's arm for support. What sort of planting had been sown up so high?

They soon reached a level patch of earth cleared of forest and planted, but not with corn or any other crop meant for food. With the stones used for marking graves. Blue-Jay could make out the names cut into the nearer stones but paused, letting Joanna rest. Runs-Far did not pause. He made straight for the nearest stone that, Blue-Jay could see from where he stood, marked where Reverend Pauling had been put into the ground long ago. But another stone nearby had caught his father's eye.

"Ah," Blue-Jay said, as his father's shoulders slumped. He did not need to read that marker to know who lay beneath it.

"He was a warrior, my Alex, and that is how he died, in battle." Joanna held to Blue-Jay's arm, gazing at Runs-Far standing alone before her husband's grave. "At King's Mountain. With him our son, David."

They stood a distance from the graves while she told of a battle even the Aniyunwiya had heard of, fought during the war between the Colonies and their King.

"When that British Colonel Ferguson threatened to lay waste our mountain settlements, the men of MacKinnon's Cove answered the call to fight. Our eldest, David and Edmund—twins—fought at their father's side. At some point in the battle Alex was shot through the lungs and fell. As he knelt over his father, David was struck in the chest by a musket ball. That's the last witness we have of them living—from Cade, who was there fighting too. It was all confusion, powder-smoke thick and choking, musket-shot tearing through autumn leaves. After the battle had ended, it was Edmund who found them. Though gravely wounded himself, Alex had lived long enough to drag

David into cover. He was propped against a tree, our son cradled in his arms."

Joanna MacKinnon closed her eyes. "Countless are the nights I've lain awake imagining their final words to one another—if they spoke any. I comfort myself thinking they would have reminded each other of what awaits us all who long for our Lord's appearing. No more death. No partings. Every tear wiped away."

"Yes." It surprised Blue-Jay that the word escaped his tightened throat. The story of Alex MacKinnon and his son was like the stories he had heard from the mouths of his own clan women the whole of his life. Desperate battles fought over some piece of ground, holding back an enemy. Fathers, uncles, brothers, sons—daughters and sisters too, for the women of his people did not all shy from battle. Warriors lauded for their bravery, praised for their daring, mourned for their passing.

At Alex MacKinnon's grave, Runs-Far sank to his knees. Blue-Jay wanted to go to his father, but Joanna spoke again, gaze roving the burial ground.

"So many loved ones gone ahead. Papa was first, a few years after we settled here. Then dear Azuba. Moses, our first miller. My sister, Charlotte. A babe of mine and Alex's who didn't live out her first year. Two of Elijah's. Others belonging to our children and theirs. Alex, David ... and Marigold," she added with a catch that spoke of fresh grief. There was a grave newer than the others, too distant for Blue-Jay to read the name inscribed upon the stone.

Joanna followed his gaze. "Mari was Elijah's wife. My dearest friend. And our cove's midwife after Azuba passed." She raised green-gray eyes to Blue-Jay, in them a depth of memory as he sometimes glimpsed in his father's gaze. Deeper, for this woman was older still. "Mari knew your mother well."

Blue-Jay's breath hitched. "As did you?"

"Oh yes—as well as I could know one of Papa's slaves. Jemma was made companion to my little sister, Charlotte, when both were girls. She was a character, your mother. Strong, stubborn, worrisome. I'm glad she left us and made a life with your father, with your people, but I missed her. So did Charlotte."

Blue-Jay looked away. "So did I."

Joanna's fingers squeezed his arm. "You weren't yet grown, were you?"

"I thought so." Blue-Jay pressed his lips tight, gaze fixed on a redbird flitting at the clearing's edge, its bright plumage making him think of Redwing. "I was twelve summers when it happened. My father was always going to talk of Creator-Jesus with those in other villages—as Reverend Pauling taught him to do. Sometimes he would stay gone many days, like other fathers who hunted meat and skins. My father hunted souls. That time I begged to go with him. My mother did not wish me to go but I thought myself too old to stay home with her and my sister."

He was surprised to hear himself spilling out the tale. Surprised as well when Joanna said, "Having raised a number of sons myself, I am inclined to agree with you."

"Had I been there when our village was raided, I might have protected my mother, kept those soldiers from taking her." That part of the story he had never spoken aloud. Not once since he and his father returned from that journey to find his mother gone. Not even to Redwing.

"You might have been old enough to travel with your father, but you weren't old enough to fight off a company of militia." Joanna's grip on his arm tightened again. "Your father has never said otherwise, has he?"

Runs-Far had never said it, but had his father thought it?

"My father has rarely spoken of my mother. Not until this journey." He hesitated, glancing down at the old woman. "I have wondered another thing..."

Joanna waited, her gaze expectant.

"I have wondered if the man who fathered me was one of those soldiers who attacked our village. If he found my mother and took her back."

Joanna shook her head. "That cannot be what happened."

Her certainty took Blue-Jay aback. "You know this? How?"

"Long before Jemma was stolen from you, that man breathed his last. He is gone past harming her, or anyone, again." Joanna studied Blue-Jay. "Do you wish to know about him? There isn't a lot I can tell but…" She trailed off, as if perceiving his answer before he spoke.

"You have told me all I wish to know of that one." *He is gone past harming her, or anyone, again.* Blue-Jay tipped his head toward the man on his knees at the graves. "My true father is that man, who honored my mother and loved her—and me as his own."

Joanna smiled, giving Blue-Jay a glimpse of the younger woman she had been. "I'm so glad Jemma had him. And you—and little Redwing. I remember Reverend Pauling telling of her birth. How is your sister?"

"She is counted among the grandmothers now."

"Goodness. Hasn't time wings?" Joanna started to say more, then frowned in concern at Runs-Far, from whom a sound had reached them. A groan.

"Granny Jo?" a voice called from behind them. Zilpha MacKinnon had come up the path.

"Come back to the house when you're ready," Joanna said. "We'll be waiting for you. As will dinner." She stepped away, crossing the ground to her son's wife.

The women left Blue-Jay and his father at the graves.

The gathering around the long table, in a room with walls painted a dark red, would have been large even without the addition of five extra—Cade, Jesse, Jeremiah Ring, Blue-Jay, and Runs-Far. It had come close to being three, though no one at the table crowded with dishes of steaming vegetables, boiled beef, and bread knew it, save Blue-Jay and his father.

Runs-Far had not appeared to hear his son's approach as he knelt before the grave of Alex MacKinnon, head bowed, rocking himself and weeping through his words: "Here I am come, yet still you have no word for me! Where is that other path? I see just the one—that same wrong one. Must I take it again?"

The outburst made Blue-Jay halt a step away from his father's bent form. Remorse had twisted his father's voice, and a crushing grief.

Another path. A wrong one. To whom did his father speak? To Alex MacKinnon or ... to Creator?

"Edo'da?"

Runs-Far sat upright, seeming surprised to find himself and Blue-Jay alone among the stones cut with the names of the dead. Above the clearing a hawk circled, stitching clouded sky to blue. At the wood's edge stood a young doe, watching them. Sunlight glistened off the tears that tracked his father's cheeks. A sight so rare as to unsettle. "Of what other path do you speak?"

His father started to rise, then reached for aid. Blue-Jay pulled him to his feet, joints creaking like trees before a wind. With his gaze on the graves, Runs-Far said, "It is time for me to tell you a thing that happened before we began this journey. Before I woke from that fever, knowing it was not my time to die. Before all that, I saw your mother."

Blue-Jay frowned. "In a dream you saw her?"

"Dream. Vision. Or maybe I crossed over and saw her in truth." Runs-Far gave a shrug that stirred the tattered fringe on his shirt. "However it was, she came to me and spoke of a path—the one I followed to this place when she was taken from us. She spoke of it dividing. She said I took the wrong fork of that path. *Turns-Around-And-Goes-Home-Without-Trying.* That is what she called me." Runs-Far's mouth twisted downward, wryness tangled in its unhappy slant. "I knew *this* for the place where that path divided. But now that I have returned to it, I do not see that other path I was meant to take. Still the help I hoped for is beyond my reach."

None of what had been said could be argued with, yet Blue-Jay found himself resisting the despair in his father's gaze. "So you will take the wrong path from this place once again?"

Anger flashed in his father's eyes. "What else is there to do?"

Something told Blue-Jay he was seeing into a corner of his father's heart he had long tried to hide. A place that healing had never reached.

As if to end the conversation, his father said, "Let us get our things from off the front of that house and go home."

It was what Blue-Jay had wanted all along to do. Why a contrary urge to argue the point arose, he could not say. "Joanna MacKinnon is waiting for us. She expects us to eat with them." It would be rude to refuse. But before Runs-Far could answer, a new thought dawned on Blue-Jay. "Is this why you stopped going on your journeys to the villages? You are angry—I see as much—but who is it you are angry with? Yourself?"

Or Creator, he thought but did not say. Though Runs-Far had taught from the Scriptures in their village until the winter day he sickened with the fever, he had never made another teaching journey after the one Blue-Jay had gone on. He hunted like other fathers while Blue-Jay tended their crops, until Redwing grew big enough to do it. "It was not your fault my mother was taken."

Fresh tears ran down his father's stony face. "It was my fault. Yet I blamed Creator. I turned back from the work He had for me to do among our people. I did not lose my faith, but I lost my heart for that good work. For that I am ashamed!"

It put his own heart on the ground, witnessing his father's brokenness. "No, Edo'da. It was not your fault." *It was mine.* Blue-Jay could not say those words either. He put a hand to his father's shoulder while the older man wept. "We will not pass a night here, but we cannot cross mountains without food in our bellies. Let us eat at Joanna MacKinnon's table, then we will start for home. Can you do that much?"

With his father in reluctant agreement, they had found their way back to Joanna's house. Cade and Jeremiah returned from the smithy with Jesse, who would hurry home after the meal. Blue-Jay assumed he and his father would accompany Jesse, though Runs-Far did not speak of it to the others.

Edmund MacKinnon, husband of Zilpha, had come home from his errand down the cove. Their son, Micah, had come in from the fields. Elijah Moon, he of the scars and missing hand, had dismissed his students. They and the women all gathered at the table, including Micah's lively red-haired wife, Sally.

Much talk went round with the dishes passed. Blue-Jay paid little heed to the English words darting around his ears like bats. He worried over his father, who stared at his plate but ate little of the food put there, despite repeated urging. Once he caught the gaze of Joanna, seated across from them. She had noticed Runs-Far's feeble appetite.

Only then did he realize the talk at one end of the table—where Edmund MacKinnon sat—had turned to Blue-Jay's mother and what might have become of her. Edmund resembled his father, Alex. He was tall and powerfully knit, with dark gold hair sun-bleached at the tailed-back ends, starting to whiten at the crown.

"Ma," he said now. "I've no notion will it be of help, but didn't Pa say there was a place downriver in the Piedmont where he and Jemma stayed, afore they crossed paths with the Cherokees—with someone he'd known back in Scotland?"

A light sprang into Joanna's gaze. She turned toward the other end of the table, where Elijah Moon sat. "A plantation, wasn't it?"

The two stared at each other, searching memories buried deep.

"Cameron," Elijah finally said.

Joanna smiled. "Yes. And that wasn't the only time Alex stayed there. He carried Reverend Pauling away from Crooked Branch's Town, on his way back to us. The reverend was ill. Alex left him there with ... *Hugh* Cameron, wasn't it?"

Edmund snapped his fingers. "Right. I can't believe I'd forgotten. Hugh Cameron was with Pa aboard that prison ship, after the '45 Rising. They met up again in Fayetteville—Cross Creek it was called then. Pa and Jemma with him."

A tremor passed through Runs-Far at the mention of their mother's slave name. His father's head had lifted.

"What was that plantation called?" Sally asked.

This time there was no pause for thought. "Mountain Laurel," Elijah said. "Alex left the reverend there before he returned to Severn."

"Severn?" Runs-Far echoed. "That is the place where Walnut was born."

"My stepfather's old plantation," Joanna said. "On the Cape Fear River."

Blue-Jay stiffened as his father asked, "How far is that place?"

"A long way." Edmund studied Runs-Far. "For you, afoot ... weeks."

"But this other," Runs-Far persisted. "Mountain Laurel. It is not so far?"

"What town's it near, Pa?" Micah asked. He was dark-haired and golden-skinned like his mother and shared the blue eyes of both parents.

"Asheborough," Edmund said. "Just a village, I think."

Micah nodded. "Not much more'n a courthouse and tavern. I went through there last summer on my way back from Hillsborough. On horseback I could reach it in two days, pushing," he added, addressing Runs-Far's question. "For you two walking...a week, I'd guess. Maybe less."

"I've not heard word of Hugh Cameron since we mustered for King's Mountain," Edmund said. "That's eighteen years ago. As for Severn, no knowing who lives there now."

It was beyond Blue-Jay's imagining, venturing eastward through North Carolina. "You are not thinking to find my mother in one of those places?" he asked his father.

The weight of every gaze around that crowded table bore into them. What each thought of the alarming notion that seemed to be forming in the very air they breathed, Blue-Jay did not know, but the despair had lifted from his father.

"I cannot answer that question," Runs-Far said. "I only know that I was wrong. There is a path left to follow. Our journey is not done."

4

CARRAWAY MOUNTAINS, NORTH CAROLINA

Had Blue-Jay held his peace about empty bellies, he and his father would not have been astride borrowed horses, having crossed the Yadkin River the night before.

Early on their third morning out from MacKinnon's Cove, east of the high mountains, they sighted a series of rugged hills and ridges rising from the lower land, greening with advancing spring, rumpled as the folds of a blanket cast aside.

"The Carraways," Edmund MacKinnon, their guide, called them.

As the track they followed plunged among them, Blue-Jay consoled himself with thinking that if they found the place called Mountain Laurel and there this doubtful path should end, Edmund would guide them straight back into their native mountains. They could go home.

Or would his father insist on journeying to that distant place where his mother had been born into slavery? *Severn.* The name alone made Blue-Jay shudder.

After the meal at the MacKinnons' table, Cade had parted with his nephew. "Sure you're easy about me and Jeremiah pushing on to Long Meadows, Jesse? I'll be a fortnight gone. No longer, can I help it."

"Zilpha and I will be on hand," old Joanna MacKinnon said. "I'll come directly, if Tamsen wants, bide with ye until the birthing."

"Or you can do as I've urged," Cade added after Joanna bid them farewell. "Bring Tamsen down to Long Meadows. But do it soon."

Cade and Jeremiah Ring had traveled with them until their path diverged north into Virginia, at which point Blue-Jay had been thankful that Edmund MacKinnon offered to accompany them to Mountain Laurel, though at first the man had tried to give directions.

"Follow the Yadkin downriver 'til just before Salisbury, where you'll want to leave it for the Cape Fear Road. That'll cross the Hillsborough Road. That takes you over the Carraways. Before you're out of 'em, a side-track shoots off toward Mountain Laurel. If you miss it and reach that new village, Asheborough . . ." Edmund must have noted the panic blooming in Blue-Jay's gaze. "Best I show you the way. I've been to Mountain Laurel—just the once, on our way to muster for King's Mountain. Hugh Cameron didn't join us. Pa never said why."

"Do you know anyone else from that place?" Runs-Far asked.

"'Twas eighteen years ago. But since we've been speaking of it, I've called to mind a woman there. Young then. A slave, I think, but definitely Indian." The memory drew Edmund's mouth up crooked. "She was a beauty. David, my twin, had buried his wife a year before and hadn't so much as looked twice at a woman, 'til he set eyes on that one. Talked of her for days."

Blue-Jay met his father's gaze. An Indian woman, young eighteen years ago. What were the chances she had any connection to them?

"After the battle," Edmund said, "losing David and Pa, I never thought about her again 'til now. Wish I could bethink me of her name."

At least Edmund MacKinnon's memory of the Carraways, with its many tracks and trails, proved sharp. It was late morning when they splashed across a shallow creek and rode their horses through an oak wood that encroached upon the rutted track cutting through it, as if no wagon had traversed it in some while. The wood soon opened upon a cleared setting, backed by a steep ridge. There was a stable and fenced paddock with a horse in it. But even to Blue-Jay's eye something about the place looked wrong.

Astride his horse in the stable yard, Edmund gave a low whistle. "The house . . . it's clean gone."

He waved a hand toward a slight rise where nothing stood but a heap of old bricks, choked with pokeberry weeds. A chestnut tree, one side of it scorched dead, grew in what must have been the dooryard. Set back from that was a whitewashed structure that might have been a cookhouse.

The place had an air of abandonment, like villages Blue-Jay had seen after the Tsalagi fled them—until a chorus of baying dogs arose. Blue-Jay tensed, seeing them loping up the track that continued past the stable toward more trees planted in flowering rows. There was no time to admire this one well-kept corner of the place before the dogs—three limp-eared hounds—were milling around the horses, making them shift and stamp.

Edmund vaulted from the saddle, his imposing presence causing the dogs to back away. "Enough! Hush now."

The dogs cringed, ceasing their baying. One, a female, beat her ropy tail against the earth. Edmund spoke gently then bent to give her head a scratch. As if that was a signal, all three dogs surged forward to sniff at Edmund's knees, wanting their ears fondled.

Blue-Jay dismounted and led their horses to the fence, where he helped Runs-Far out of the saddle. The horse in the paddock ambled over to greet their mounts. As his father steadied himself on the earth, a voice called from down the track.

"Halloo there!"

A white man in tattered trousers and fringed hunting shirt had come into view, trotting along the track that passed the stable. He was wiry and small, neither young nor old, wearing a battered hat with a limp brim and toting a rifle, though he did not aim it their way.

Blue-Jay and Runs-Far held back, letting Edmund advance to meet this welcome.

The man gave his name as Charlie Spencer. He had some knowledge of MacKinnon's Cove, more so of Cade and Jesse when Edmund mentioned various neighbors of the MacKinnons.

"Did me some trapping Overmountain in the Watauga—what they're calling Tennessee now. Crossed paths with Cade and Jesse. Ten, eleven years back."

When Charlie Spencer raised a questioning brow at Blue-Jay and Runs-Far, Edmund gave their names then asked, "What's become of this place, and Hugh Cameron, who owned it—last my family knew?"

"Well, sir." Charlie Spencer scratched a bristled cheek. "The house come down in a fire, autumn of '94. Hugh Cameron perished in the conflagration—left the place to his nephew."

Runs-Far's dismay at the news was all but palpable. Yet another link to Blue-Jay's mother gone beyond their reach.

"I'm sorry to hear it," Edmund said. "Is Cameron's nephew about? I don't know if he'll have answers, but we've questions to put to him, these men and I." He nodded at Runs-Far—meaning to tell him not to give up hope?

Charlie Spencer shook his head. "Afraid not. Sold the place nigh two years back. Lit out for ... parts north." The man studied their faces. "Don't know what questions ye might've had for the Camerons, but maybe John Reynold could help ye. He owns this land now. I'm his hired man, living in the old overseer cabin." He canted his head down the track from whence he had come. "Yonder."

"This Reynold," Blue-Jay said. "Did he know those here before? Did he know Hugh Cameron or his nephew?"

"Aye. He and his wife were fast friends with Ian Cameron—the nephew. Still are."

"And with those he enslaved?"

"Reckon some more'n others."

Blue-Jay felt strangely out of breath. "Do you remember one, a woman of Indian blood?"

Charlie pushed his hat up on his brow, blue eyes sparking. He sucked on his teeth while his hounds sniffed about. Finally he said, "Reckon I'll let John answer your questions. He's to home today. Got a project out in the barn keeping him busy."

Blue-Jay had not missed that spark at mention of an Indian woman. He did not think his father had either.

"We've come this far," Edmund said. "Might as well meet the man. He's nearby?"

"Yes sir. He was neighbor to the Camerons afore he bought what was left of Mountain Laurel here. Still lives on his homestead, off through the wood a step." Charlie Spencer grinned, showing gaps where his eyeteeth were missing. "Dogs and I got nothing pressing. We'll walk ye on over."

The wife of John Reynold met them on the porch of a house built of square-hewed logs. Attached to it was an open area with a floor and roof connecting it to a smaller cabin, fresh with the look of new-cut wood. To judge from the smoking chimney and the smells coming from its open door, it was the cookhouse for this family.

The woman, who Charlie Spencer called Cecily, had a girl-child cradled to her hip, a babe of ten or eleven moons wearing a loose, rumpled garment. Cecily Reynold surveyed the crowd—man, dog, and horse—clustered in her yard, looking mildly amused. "Who are these you bring to my door, Charlie?"

She was a slender woman, fair-skinned, with dark hair pinned up from a delicate face, not at all rumpled in a skirt the blue of a kingfisher's wing. She was also French, like the traders that still sometimes came to the Aniyunwiya from their places in the west, evident the instant she had spoken.

While his dogs wandered toward the barn with the ease of animals accustomed to that place, Charlie Spencer named Edmund MacKinnon of MacKinnon's Cove, who bowed with his hat removed and took up the task of naming Blue-Jay and Runs-Far. "They've come a mighty distance in search of Hugh Cameron, who we learn has passed. His nephew's gone away north, leaving your husband in possession of his lands. They've questions they hoped Mr. Reynold—or yourself, ma'am—might still answer."

Surprise sharpened Cecily Reynold's gaze. "Questions about the Camerons?"

"Yes ma'am," Charlie said. "John out to the barn?"

A dark-haired boy had appeared in the barn's doorway to greet the hounds. At sight of strange men and horses in his yard, he ducked back inside, calling to someone therein.

Cecily Reynold's dark eyes sparkled. "John should be out to us presently."

The horses were watered and fed. With his coat smelling of wood shavings, John Reynold, brown of hair and eye, another English-born, joined them in the covered space between the cabins—he called it a *dogtrot*—where they sat on benches with their bags and rifles set nearby, and a plate of sugared bread made into small loaves that Blue-Jay, though hungry, found too sweet for his liking, but which better pleased his father. The boy played in the yard with the dogs. Cecily Reynold and her girl-child returned to whatever task their arrival had interrupted, inside the cabin, while Edmund repeated the nature of their journey and the question Blue-Jay had voiced to Charlie.

"An Indian woman?" John Reynold replied. "Lily, do you mean?"

Beside Blue-Jay on a bench, Runs-Far jerked at the speaking of the name.

"Lily. That might have been her." Edmund shifted to face Blue-Jay and Runs-Far. "The woman my brother was taken with."

"Your brother?" John Reynold's question prompted Edmund's telling of his twin and their brief visit to Mountain Laurel years ago, before the battle in which that brother died.

Blue-Jay waited for the story to be told then, when his father remained silent, hands fisted on his knees, asked, "Will you tell us of this one you call Lily?"

John Reynold studied Runs-Far and, seeming to understand the import of his words, gentled his tone. "To tell you Lily's story, I need to start with her mother. This was long before Cecily and I came to these shores. We had the story from Mountain Laurel's slaves, some who were here at the time of the old French war, when soldiers came back from fighting in the mountains. A militia unit stopped at Mountain Laurel with a woman in tow, taken from a Cherokee village. A woman who spoke no English. They left her at Mountain Laurel—sold her to the mistress there at the time. Hugh Cameron's first wife. They thought the woman a runaway slave, a mixed-blood, one who had lived among your people long enough to learn your ways."

A runaway slave. A woman of mixed blood. A stone felt lodged in Blue-Jay's throat, making it hard to speak. "This woman was with child?"

"She was. And died birthing the child—Lily. Was she someone you knew?"

At last his father spoke, his voice thick with shock. "I believe she was my wife. Mother to this one." He rested a hand on Blue-Jay's shoulder. "Was she called Sedi?"

"Sedi?" John frowned. "The folk at Mountain Laurel thought she was calling herself *Sadie.*"

His father's hand slipped from his shoulder. Runs-Far's head bowed forward until it nearly touched his knees.

Blue-Jay shook his head. "*Sedi.* Walnut, you would say." He could not look at his father's bent form. "She is dead then, my mother."

All gathered under that dogtrot were silent. Blue-Jay touched his father's back. Runs-Far did not straighten. Instead he reached for his bag, lying on the boards at his feet. He opened its flap and plunged his hand within.

"Edo'da?" Blue-Jay said with an aching heart. "Is there something you need?"

"These." His father sat up, eyes moist, something clasped in his hand. He opened his fingers to reveal a pair of moccasins worked in red and white beads. Moccasins for the tiniest of feet. Blue-Jay had never seen them before.

"Did my mother make those?"

Runs-Far nodded. "For the child that was coming."

A child who never wore them.

"I'm sorry." John Reynold reached out, placing a hand on Runs-Far's. "But you need to know, the child, Lily, is very much alive. We had a letter only last week. I think—"

"Here it is, *mon cher.*" Cecily stepped from the cabin with a much-folded piece of paper—one of the talking papers, *letters*, his father had often exchanged with Reverend Pauling—in hand. "I fetched this as soon as I heard the reason for your visitation. Oh…" Catching sight of the moccasins, she crossed to Runs-Far. "Are they not the sweetest things?"

Blue-Jay's heart thumped as he and his father stared at the woman and the letter she held. There was something of a dream to this, the cabin, these people, their answers to the questions he, his father, and Redwing had so long desired to ask. He heard his own voice say, "Is that from … that one you named? From Lily?"

"It is from her daughter," Cecily replied. "My dear friend who I miss very much."

His father grunted like a man arrow-shot to the chest. Blue Jay gripped his arm. "This Lily has a daughter?"

"*Certainement.* Seona, she is called. And Seona has a son, Gabriel."

Lily. Seona. Gabriel. Blue-Jay turned the names over in his mind, unable to think past them.

"Where?" The word burst from Runs-Far like a raven's croak. "Where is my daughter and her family?"

"*Tsigalili,*" Cecily blurted in her turn, then pressed a hand to her throat. "It has just come to mind. That is the name given by Lily's mother. By … how did you call her—Walnut?"

Runs-Far groaned. Blue-Jay caught a glaze of pain in his father's eyes before Runs-Far slumped against him. The tiny moccasins tumbled to the dogtrot's floor planks.

5

His father lay unconscious on a bed in the Reynolds' cabin. Not struck ill again or sleeping from exhaustion, though this journey had proved wearisome enough. At least Blue-Jay did not think so. He rather thought his father slept by an act of his will, as if this news of a daughter, granddaughter, and great-grandson was too much to absorb, along with learning Blue-Jay's mother had died in that place so long ago.

Cecily Reynold had put the moccasins next to the bed, resting atop his father's bag. They looked as they must have the day his mother finished them and tucked them away to await tiny feet they never would enclose.

The others had gathered out under the dogtrot, save the boy. He hung at the door, peering into the room, until his mother called him away. Blue-Jay heard their murmurs but paid them little heed, until Edmund MacKinnon asked, "What does it mean, Tsigalili?"

Before the chorus of *I don't knows* ended, Blue-Jay stepped from the cabin. All gazes swung to him. "My mother gave her children bird-names. Blue-Jay for me. My sister, Redwing. Now this other one. I do not recall your word. It is a small bird with…" He spread a hand over his head. "Black on top, like a cap."

"A chickadee?" Charlie Spencer guessed.

Blue-Jay nodded. "I think so."

"Lily always wondered at its meaning," Cecily said. "*Lily* is a shortening of Tsigalili."

"Where is she now?" Blue-Jay asked. "Where is Lily?"

The smiles of all but Edmund MacKinnon faltered.

"You hesitate to say? Is she a slave to Ian Cameron, this one you say went away north somewhere? Did he take my sister to serve him?"

It was John Reynold who answered. "It's a long story, and rather complicated. Lily and Seona were both enslaved at Mountain Laurel when Ian came here, from his parents' home in Boston, to become his uncle's heir."

Boston was a name Blue-Jay had heard, though where such a place might be, he did not know. "When was this that he came here?"

"Five years back, come autumn," Charlie said.

Cecily took up the tale. "Though she was the slave of Hugh Cameron—the uncle—Ian grew to love Seona but then ... much harm was done by those wishing to part them. It is a long story, as John has said, with much heartache woven through it."

"Before the house burned," John said, "Hugh Cameron arranged for Lily and Seona to be manumitted—freed—a thing Ian wanted to see done as well. After the fire, and learning Hugh had freed them before he died, Lily and Seona went to live in Boston, with Ian's parents. Seona's son, Gabriel, went with them."

Blue-Jay struggled to keep straight all the names and happenings, but his head felt like a cobwebby lodge in need of sweeping. "Gabriel? Who was that one's father?"

"Ian Cameron, *sans doute*," Cecily said.

That was unexpected. "Then why did he send the woman he loved, and their son, to this Boston?"

"Couple reasons," Charlie said. "For one, freed slaves can't stay in North Carolina. That's a law. And two, Ian had gone and married Judith, one of his uncle stepdaughters, by then. So he sent Seona and Gabriel, Lily too, up to Boston while he stayed at Mountain Laurel with Judith, living in the cabin that's mine now. 'Least that's what he did for a time..."

Charlie trailed into awkward silence, in which Blue-Jay absorbed his words with little of the cobwebs cleared, but a growing indignation. "You are telling me that Ian Cameron loved my sister's daughter but sent her away, made another his wife? Where is he now?"

Cecily began to speak, then her gaze shifted, drawn across the cabin yard to the barn. "*Mon cher.* Thomas is returned, but I do not see—" As if she had misspoken, she clapped a hand across her mouth.

Blue-Jay glimpsed a black man, of average height but broad of shoulder, dressed in coat and breeches and a hat that shadowed his features, ducking into the barn. Though Cecily seemed flustered by whatever slip of tongue she had made about the man, John merely stood with his head cocked to the side, as if to catch a sound in the nearby forest.

Long ago, before Blue-Jay's mother was taken, Runs-Far had often sat in such listening stillness. Blue-Jay knew what it meant. John was hearing from Creator.

At last he spoke. "It's all right, Cecily. I don't for a moment think it a coincidence, these three arriving on this, of all days. I think it safe to tell them."

Though Blue-Jay did not understand his meaning, Cecily took her hand from her mouth but cast an uncertain glance at Edmund MacKinnon. John cleared his throat to address the man. "I must ask you, sir. Do you or your kin enslave any man, woman, or child?"

Edmund's dark gold eyebrows drifted high. "Nary a one. Matter of fact, some of my wife's kin were manumitted slaves."

John gave a nod. "Keep the children here," he told his wife, then to Blue-Jay and Edmund said, "Come out to the barn with me and Charlie, if you will. There's someone you need to meet."

When Charlie had first mentioned John Reynold, he had spoken of a project the man had been working on in his barn. That turned out to be a wagon, over the bed of which John was fitting a second bed, leaving a space about a forearm's length in height between the two. Blue-Jay had seen wagons before, even driven one, but had never seen one constructed like this.

Leaving Blue-Jay and Edmund standing by the wagon, John and Charlie went deeper into the horse-smelling barn—to find the one Cecily had called *Thomas*, Blue-Jay supposed, wherever he was hiding himself. Blue-Jay was distracted by thoughts of his father, asleep in this family's cabin. Would Runs-Far be able to ride from that place any time soon?

He was thinking also of his mother, whose life had ended back along the path they had followed, at the place called Mountain Laurel by the Camerons, who had lived there.

He was thinking of the sister he had not known about until moments ago—Chickadee—and her daughter, and that daughter's son. And he was thinking about Ian Cameron, who had sent them away to Boston and was gone now himself. Exactly where, Blue-Jay had yet to hear.

"He loved my sister's daughter, they had a child... but he married another?"

He could not get his mind around it and did not realize he had muttered aloud until Edmund said, "Doesn't speak well of the man, I grant you. But it's not the first I've heard the like. Guess you'll need to find this Ian Cameron to know for certain. Maybe head next for Boston, where the others were sent."

Before Blue-Jay could say he had no intention of traveling to Boston or anywhere else except back to the mountains of their home, an unfamiliar voice spoke behind him.

"If you're talking of Ian Cameron, you're too late to find him in Boston. He's moved on from there."

The man called Thomas strode from the barn's shadows, John and Charlie behind him. He was younger than Blue-Jay had thought him from a distance. Not yet thirty summers and well-made in face and frame. Yet there was about his African features the worn, wary visage of one who had seen and survived danger. Illness too. His dark eyes were shadowed with both, their whites tinged a yellowish cast. He was introduced as Thomas Ross.

"You know Ian Cameron?" Blue-Jay asked.

Thomas Ross grinned, showing good teeth, white against his full lips. "Friends since we were boys. First in Boston, then over at Mountain Laurel. But what's your interest in Ian Cameron?"

John explained. "This man's called Blue-Jay. He's Lily's brother. He and his father, a Cherokee elder called Runs-Far, were hoping to find news of Lily's mother. And they have."

Thomas removed his hat to run a hand over black hair cropped close like a cap. "I know the story, that woman the old mistress took in. Lily's mama. Seona's grandmama. I didn't know her, of course, but Lily and Seona I came to know reasonably well."

Questions leapt to Blue-Jay's tongue. So many he had to sort through them all to find the one most needing answered. "You say that Ian Cameron was in Boston but is not now. Where then is he? Are my sister and the others of my blood with him?"

"Nigh on two years back, according to Seona, Ian lit out for a place in New York. Shiloh, it's called. As to whether she and Lily are with him now or still in Boston, I couldn't say."

"I can," John said. "Seona, Lily, and Gabriel made the journey west to New York last year. They've settled in Shiloh, with Ian and the others. At his farm."

Blue-Jay had been about to ask what *others*, but Thomas spoke first. "I saw Lily and Seona in Boston, a few months before they must have up and left. Seona told me about Shiloh, enough so as I could find it. In fact, I've reason to—"

John cleared his throat. "Thomas, I'd speak with you and Charlie a moment. If you'll pardon us again?" he said to Edmund and Blue-Jay.

While the three stepped deeper into the barn, Blue-Jay was still scrambling to make sense of a tale doled out in mouthfuls. Why would Lily and her daughter go to Ian Cameron, who sent them away before? What of the man's wife, that one called Judith? Where was she? What sort of people was his sister linked to, in this place called Shiloh?

He studied the three men, obscured by the barn's shadows, and was surprised to see their heads bowed together, as if in prayer. Something of importance was taking place there. Or about to. The hairs on Blue-Jay's arms rose beneath the checked sleeves of his shirt as the three finished praying and rejoined them.

"All right," Thomas said, as one who takes authority. "Here's what's happening. I plan to drive this wagon north out of Carolina, up through Virginia, Maryland, Pennsylvania—all the way to Shiloh, New York, as it happens."

"What are you carrying?" Edmund asked, though a glance at his face made Blue-Jay think he had guessed.

"A girl. Name of Esther. A slave at Chesterfield Plantation, not far from here."

"That's why John's working on this wagon here," Charlie said.

"We'll keep her hidden." Thomas nodded at the space being enclosed with the false bed, then met Blue-Jay's gaze. "You and your father are welcome to travel with us, if you want to."

All eyes turned to Blue-Jay, who stood mute, unable to grasp what was being offered.

"I cannot guarantee we won't be pursued," Thomas added. "Chesterfield's master, Gideon Pryce, isn't one to cross. But it's time for Esther to make her exodus and Shiloh is her promised land. Will you go with us?"

More names. More places. Overwhelmed by it all, Blue-Jay sputtered, "M-my father is old. He has been ill. And there will be dangers, more than just pursuit."

"*Many dangers toils and snares,*" Charlie interjected. "Like the song says. God's grace has brought Thomas safe thus far."

"Reckon His grace will lead me home again," Thomas finished. "Lead us all home."

Home. With a tongue gone dry Blue-Jay said, "How will you make it so far?"

"One step at a time." Thomas seemed undaunted by the distance he had described. "I know places, people who will help us. I've made this journey before—or ones like it. But the Carolina state line isn't our first hurdle to jump."

Our first hurdle? Blue-Jay had not said he would have any part of this. Surely his father would see such a journey was beyond him to make, once he was told of it—if he must be told at all.

"What is your first hurdle?" Edmund asked.

John put his hand on Thomas's shoulder, as Charlie grinned and said, "Getting Esther shed of Chesterfield. This very night."

CHESTERFIELD PLANTATION

They waited at the wood's edge for darkness to fall before creeping out with a rising mist to cross unsown fields. A track led them past a silent sawmill, then drew them ever closer to the plantation's main dwelling, until that structure loomed in the darkness. Far too close for comfort.

The girl was to meet them at the cooperage, a place Thomas Ross knew. He and Charlie Spencer had slipped along a row of wooden structures that, Blue-Jay was told, were the shops where slaves worked during the day. They left Blue-Jay crouched at the far end, pressed against a building that smelled of sheep's wool and dye-plants.

No slaves slept in the shops, Thomas has assured him. But if anyone stirred or came poking around Blue-Jay was to do one of two things. He could hurl a rock—he clutched one for the purpose—and make a clatter in a different direction to draw attention away from the cooperage, then hurry down the shadowed lane to tell the others to go another way. Or he could give an agreed upon warning, the call of the barred-tailed owl. Then he was to get himself away, back to the sawmill and across the fields to the forest. Hunkered in the humid dark, sweating despite the night's cool, Blue-Jay asked Creator to spare him having to find his way back to the Reynolds' farm on his own.

They had set out on foot before the sun was down, passing through forest, over a low ridge, then across a creek that had soaked Blue-Jay's moccasins when he slipped on a log. Not a short distance. As his heart slammed at thought of getting himself away from this place without being shot or set upon by dogs, he tried to unravel how he had gotten himself into this situation.

The girl they were stealing away, he had learned, was known to Chickadee and her daughter.

"Esther was like a younger sister to Seona," John Reynold had explained. "She was enslaved not to Ian or his uncle, but to Lucinda Cameron, his uncle's wife. When the house burned and Hugh Cameron died, Lucinda took Esther and the girl's parents to Chesterfield, where her daughter, Rosalyn Pryce, is mistress. Esther serves now as Rosalyn's personal maid."

"She'll be waiting for us," Thomas said. "I got word to her. But we could use another set of eyes to be on the lookout."

Blue-Jay, slow to realize this last statement was directed at him, gaped at the younger man.

"John cannot be seen helping," Thomas added, "else his home and aid would be compromised—at the very least. We don't intend Esther to be the last in these parts I lead to freedom. I need John where he is."

Blue-Jay had no memory of saying he would help, though he supposed he must have. He did recall asking whether John gave any credit to Creator's words against stealing another man's property. John was convinced he obeyed a higher law, that no man had the right to hold another in bondage. "I'll continue to act upon that conviction as long I'm able. Then, if I must, I'll find another place to settle. But while I'm here, I'll do my part to set the captives free."

Things after that had happened fast. John and Charlie finished their work on the wagon, Edmund remaining in the barn with them. Cecily tended her children and cooked much food—some meant for Thomas and the girl to take with them, should their plans succeed. Runs-Far slept on. Blue-Jay had stood by his father's sleeping form, certain that even if he helped free the girl, he and his father would not make the journey to Shiloh. They would go back to the mountains with Edmund MacKinnon, who would wait until morning to start for home.

Thomas Ross frightened Blue-Jay. While he admired the younger man's courage and conviction, such reckless daring was a thing to get him killed. Blue-Jay would not bring his father into peril by traveling with the man. Not even to find his unknown sister... though crouched in the dark of a strange plantation, he could not banish the image of tiny moccasins made by his mother's clever hands.

At least there was no sign of other slaves awake to cry alarm, if that was what another slave would do. Blue-Jay did not know much about the slaves of the *unega*—the white man. Some of the Aniyunwiya kept slaves, but not in his village. It was a thing their peace chiefs had spoken against all the seasons Reverend Pauling, and after him, Runs-Far, had taught from Creator's book. Those seasons were many.

Blue-Jay thought as did John Reynold. No man should own another.

Now he breathed the night air and smelled the well-trodden earth of that place where one man, Gideon Pryce, owned many. Smelled its stinks, animal and human. Clouds had come up to cover parts of the sky, still admitting patchy starlight. He prayed this would be over quick. That Thomas and the girl could take that wagon out of John Reynold's barn and be gone.

He heard them coming before he saw the shapes of two men creeping like shadows along the shops, behind them the smaller form of a girl nearly grown, not the child Blue-Jay had been picturing. She wore a boy's knee breeches, skinny shins and feet bare below, a dark, loose-fitting coat, with a hat on her head like a man would wear, its brim wide. She was tugging at Thomas's coattail, the sound of her voice a hissing in the night.

Thomas tried to shush her, but the girl would not be quieted.

"Listen!" she whispered as soon as Charlie verified all was well at that end of the shop row. "I'm trying to tell you—Miss Rosalyn weren't in her bed. Afore I crept out, I checked."

Thomas clapped a hand across the girl's mouth. "She'll have been with Pryce." He spoke so low Blue-Jay barely caught the words, while Charlie scanned their route back toward the sawmill. "Be glad she was."

The girl's head wagged back and forth, eyes white-rimmed above Thomas's muffling hand.

Charlie beckoned them around the last shop in the row. Eager to be gone from that place, Blue-Jay stood and followed, hearing the scuff of feet on earth behind him as Thomas urged the girl forward.

That was as far as they got.

It was the woman's fair hair, down off her head in a long braid, that Blue-Jay glimpsed first, before the shawl-wrapped figure stepped across their path. A voice, sharp and loud in the night, froze them.

"Where on God's earth are you bound, Esther, in that ridiculous costume? And who are these helping you away?"

6

"Miss Rosalyn . . ." Esther moaned, then turned on Thomas. "I *told* you she weren't in her bed!"

"You are correct, Esther. But surely you aren't taking your leave without introducing your friends?" The woman Blue-Jay understood to be the girl's mistress, Rosalyn Pryce, drew near enough to taint the air with liquored breath. "Though it seems I am acquainted with one already. Thomas Ross, up to old tricks, I see. And is that Charlie Spencer with you?"

When Charlie said nothing, the woman's gaze shifted to Blue-Jay. She drew in a breath, stepping closer to better see him. "Ian Cameron?"

A hand shot out from the shawl, gripping Blue-Jay's arm. The touch chilled through his shirtsleeve.

"Not Ian." Releasing him, Rosalyn Pryce's gaze swept Blue-Jay from moccasins to leggings to the tomahawk and knife that hung at his belt. "Yet near as may be, whatever you are. Some sort of half-breed? *He* was—at heart."

Leaving Blue-Jay baffled as to why she should mistake him for Ian Cameron, the woman dismissed him, her focus returning to the girl.

"Is it to my sister's husband you're bound? No—" She raised a hand before the girl could reply. "Don't. I cannot tell what I don't know. But Esther, whatever would your mama say, could she see you now?"

"I wish I knew!" Esther blurted.

Her mistress's voice was a mockery of kindness. "Yes. We were all saddened by your mama's death, coming so soon after your daddy was sold. Carried down to Georgia, I heard."

The girl's muffled sobs troubled the silence. Then Thomas spoke, voice edged with something just shy of disdain. "What are you doing out here, Mrs. Pryce?"

"Let 'em go, Miss Rosalyn," Esther pleaded. "I'll go back to my pallet. Don't let Mister Gideon catch 'em."

Ignoring her, Rosalyn Pryce fixed Thomas in her gaze. "You ask what I'm doing out here—and think you know. Well, you don't. I'm here to see Esther makes her escape."

"*What*?" Esther breathed.

Her mistress turned on her. "Do you think me blind, girl? I've seen how Gideon's looked at you lately."

Esther's swallow was audible. "He—Master Gideon ain't never..."

"Not yet?" Bitterness laced the woman's words as a pungent bark of laughter widened her mouth. "Good. Though I am resigned to seeing his ill-begotten progeny playing in the dirt of the slave quarter, he will not—God as my witness—have *you*. Nor you him," she added in an undertone.

The stunned silence seemed to last an eternity before Thomas asked, "You won't tell him?"

"I shall not need to. He'll hear of it soon enough. How you use what time my silence buys, that is your concern."

Needing no further prompting, Charlie Spencer grasped Blue-Jay's arm and tugged him toward the track to the mill. Away from that hateful place.

Behind him the girl choked out, "Thank you, Miss Rosalyn."

"Spare me your gratitude," came the reply. "I don't do this for *you*. It pleases me to think Gideon won't get what he wants—for once. So hadn't you best fly, little bird?"

Blue-Jay glanced back to see Thomas and the girl following, beyond them the solitary figure of Chesterfield's mistress. She took a few steps after them and spoke, voice cold.

"Thomas—if you see him, give Ian a message from me. Tell him... tell him he was right."

Thomas paused, turning back to the woman standing alone in the dark. "About what?"

"He will know." Rosalyn Pryce drew the ends of her shawl tighter around herself. "But also tell him this: I have not forgiven him for breaking my sister's heart. I never will."

Esther sniffled and wiped at tears until they reached John Reynold's farm. Cecily met them in the lantern-lit barn, ready to comfort and provision the girl for the journey in the wagon these people hoped would carry her to freedom.

Thomas told Cecily of their encounter with Rosalyn Pryce. Charlie rounded up his dogs and vanished into the night. Bound for home, Blue-Jay supposed. Of his father, John Reynold, or Edmund MacKinnon, there was no sign. Nor were Edmund's horses in the boxes where Blue-Jay had last seen them.

"Mr. MacKinnon has gone," Cecily said when he interrupted her talk with Thomas to ask. "He left not long after you. There was daylight to spare, you see."

Blue-Jay did not see. "He left? Without me and my father?"

"It was your father's wish. He woke after you left for Chesterfield. John told him what was happening. Your father read Seona's letter. Then he told Mr. MacKinnon to go back to his home in the mountains."

Blue-Jay stared. "Where is my father now?"

Cecily had an arm around Esther, who was nearly as tall as the Frenchwoman. "Your father slept again after Mr. MacKinnon's departure, only to awaken and insist upon seeing the place where Lily and Seona lived. The old slave cabins at Mountain Laurel. John took him there, not very long ago."

Esther's dark eyes were huge in the lanternlight, the rest of her face pinched and frightened under her wide-brimmed hat. Blue-Jay felt her tension, but his head spun now with his own fears. "Where are these cabins? Back down that trail we came along from the place where the house burned?"

"That's right," Thomas said. "Can you find it?"

Blue-Jay nodded. "I remember the way. Even in darkness I will find it."

"But is there time?" Cecily asked.

Thomas's mouth twisted. "Rosalyn said she wouldn't tell Pryce. We've the night, maybe longer, before they start hunting."

Cecily did not look reassured. "Do you trust the woman to keep her word?"

"I trust the spite I heard in her. She'll hold her peace." Thomas nodded to Blue-Jay. "Find your father. We'll meet you on the road. John knows where."

We'll meet you on the road. What did Thomas mean, speaking as though Blue-Jay had agreed to journey with them? He felt as much urgency to be gone from that place as Esther must be feeling, but for his own reason. He meant to get his father back on that road in hope of overtaking Edmund MacKinnon, who he hoped would not have traveled too great a distance before stopping to sleep. If they walked through what remained of the night, by morning they should have found him. And his horses.

Blue-Jay had taken up his and his father's bags and his rifle, said his good-byes, and sprinted for the trail that had brought him to that farm. He took no means of lighting his way through the night-chilling wood.

Even in darkness I will find it.

But what of the path he and his father had followed these past weeks? Would it not have been better never to know what happened to his mother, never learned of a sister, than to stir up a grief so strong it had all but felled his father into a stranger's bed? Better never to prod at old wounds to find them still so raw.

Desperate for wisdom, for strength to make a hard choice if his father proved unreasonable, he prayed to Creator as he blundered through spiders' webs spun across the trail since his father's passing, several times catching a toe on a root, coming near to falling.

Emerging from the woods to see the structure he had earlier taken for a cookhouse, he paused to catch his breath, sucking in the damp air. From somewhere in the forest he had passed through, a barred owl gave the call he had not needed to use at Chesterfield.

Who-cooks-for-you? Who-cooks-for-you-all?

That was what his father once said the unega thought that owl was saying. The Tsalagi knew different. But there stood that old cookhouse, shut up and abandoned. Had his sister done the cooking within its walls for the people who enslaved her? Those Camerons.

Thrusting away thoughts of that faceless one, no more substantial than a ghost, Blue-Jay loped past the structure to the lane that ran by the stable. He wanted to call out to his father but hesitated to do so.

One of Charlie Spencer's soft-eared dogs coming out of the dark gave him such a fright he yelped. The dog snuffled its cold nose at his hand, then turned and trotted down the lane. Blue-Jay followed, passing a cabin where the other dogs lay curled by the door. From a window a candle's light glowed. Charlie's cabin?

Blue-Jay was about to approach it when voices reached him, coming from a nearby grove of oak trees. He paused, gazing into their shadows, listening, then made his way along the track littered with leaves and last year's acorns, until he could see the shapes of smaller cabins. Two, set close. The door of one, which had been pulled shut, creaked open in response to a breeze that rustled new leaves above. From within spilled a lantern's wavering light. When no one emerged, Blue-Jay crept close and listened to the conversation going on inside. His father was speaking.

"…and that was the last journey I made to share the love of Creator-Jesus with my people not living in my own village. I have many times turned back from journeys I was meant to make, refusing Creator's call on my heart, starting with the journey I took to search for my wife. Perhaps I would have much sooner learned about my daughter, had I not given up when I did, at the grave of Reverend Pauling."

Blue-Jay stood gripping his rifle and the packs, startled by his father's words. Runs-Far did not sound aggrieved by the things they had learned. Regretful, yes. But there was a quality to his voice Blue-Jay had seldom heard since coming home to the grief of his mother vanished from their lives. What he was hearing was *joy*.

"Creator is merciful. He gives an old man this miracle—a daughter living—here at the end when that man thought all was finished, and so much lost."

Miracle. Blue-Jay knew the word's meaning. He had heard the stories of Creator-Jesus, the wonders performed when he walked among men long ago. Walking on water. Multiplying food to feed thousands. Opening blind eyes. Raising the dead. He could not see how to apply the word to what his father was talking about.

"I can see there is a call on your heart now," John Reynold said. "What will you do?"

"I have a daughter, Chickadee, called Lily by those who love her. I have a granddaughter, Seona. A great-grandson, Gabriel." His father's voice swelled with strength as he spoke the names. "I cannot undo the past. I cannot make the journeys I should have made over all the years. But I can finish this one."

Blue-Jay caught his breath. Their journey *was* complete. They had learned what happened to his mother after the soldiers carried her off. Yes, there was a sister, but the distance that sister had traveled away from this place was vast. And his father was old. Only weeks ago he had been dying.

"There's one thing you need to know," John said. "Seona didn't mention it in the letter you read, but Lily was wed last autumn—to a Mohawk man from Canada. She went with him to his people, to a place called Grand River. I believe she meant to return to Shiloh, but I don't know when that will be."

"Canada? That is a longer distance than New York, I think."

"By a few days travel at least."

Relief flooded Blue-Jay. The distance between them and this unknown sister, already great, had just increased.

So had his father's determination. "There is still one thing I can do for my wife, who died in this place birthing our daughter. Creator willing and lending me strength, I will do it. But first I will find my granddaughter. I will find Seona."

"You'll travel with Thomas then?" John asked while in the dark outside the cabin Blue-Jay's jaw hung slack. "You and your son?"

"We will," said his father.

"I'd hoped you would. Blue-Jay could pass for a white man. Would he be willing to drive the wagon during the day? Thomas can play the slave. He's practiced the art."

"I am sure my son can do this. Here I will wait, if you will hurry back to your farm and tell—"

"Edo'da, I am here—and cannot believe what I am hearing!"

Blue-Jay had no memory of pushing his way into the cabin where the two were hatching their impossible plan. Of slinging down the bags and setting his rifle against a wall. He was suddenly standing in the lanternlight, gaze darting into cobwebby corners, to leaves littering packed earth, a clay hearth crumbling, two narrow wooden frames that must have been beds. His sister's? Her daughter's?

Then his gaze fastened on his father's face, a countenance he hardly recognized. The joy he had heard in his father's voice overflowed the features that welcomed his appearing—and frightened the English clean out of Blue-Jay's head.

"What do you mean by making these decisions without me?" he asked in Tsalagi. "We are not going to New York. We are going home. If we hurry, we can overtake Edmund MacKinnon and his horses. Why would you send him away?"

Runs-Far's smile dimmed at this outburst. Perhaps to keep the fact of Blue-Jay's disrespect between them, he also spoke in the language of their people. "My son, calm yourself. We may find Edmund Mackinnon, and he may let us ride his horses yet a while, but I will not travel back to MacKinnon's Cove with him. I will go north, with Thomas and the girl he is rescuing. I will go to Shiloh. I hope you will come with me."

Blue-Jay stepped close to his father and lowered his voice. "No, Edo'da. It is too far. There is too much danger on that path."

"But we have a plan, this man and I." Runs-Far tilted his whitened head toward John Reynold, watching them and making no effort to hide it.

"I heard that plan. It is not a good one!"

John cleared his throat. "I heard you mention MacKinnon's name. Thomas will be taking the same road, at first. You'll travel faster in that wagon than on foot, have a better chance of overtaking the man—if that's what you resolve to do."

Runs-Far nodded. "This is true."

"It is," Blue-Jay admitted, reverting to English. "But I do not mean to ride to New York in that wagon. Not with men coming to take back the girl and put a rope around our necks, or whatever they do to slave-stealers." Seeing his father about to protest, he raised a hand. "For this one night I will agree to it. Until we overtake Edmund MacKinnon."

Runs-Far set his jaw, returning Blue-Jay's stare. "I am going to Shiloh in New York State. That is where the girl wishes to go—this one's wife told me so." He placed a hand on John's shoulder. "She wishes to live with my granddaughter and her husband."

This was the first Blue-Jay could remember anyone mentioning a husband of Seona, his sister's daughter. "Who is that?"

"Ian Cameron," John Reynold said.

Blue-Jay's lip curled. "I have heard nothing of that one to make me wish to meet him. We can discuss this later, Edo'da." His gaze fastened on John. "Thomas says you know where on the road we are to meet the wagon. Will you show us the way?"

The rattle of wagon wheels met their ears seconds after they reached the road, leaving no space for more discussion. Thomas caught sight of them on the verge and pulled the horses to a halt. John Reynold took something from his coat and pressed it into Blue-Jay's hand.

"A letter. To Ian Cameron. Please take it," John said when Blue-Jay's impulse was to refuse the thing. "Give it to Thomas if you part ways. If not... I would ask that you put this into Ian's hands for me. Will you do that?"

The thing given him felt thicker than a mere letter to Blue-Jay, who had seen the talking papers carried over mountains by various hands, sent to his father from the Reverend Pauling and others, many years ago. John Reynold must have meant for Thomas to take the parcel north. But Thomas was busy helping Runs-Far into the wagon's bed, where Esther must already be hidden. There was no sign of her. Only the dim shapes of barrels and crates. Containing what, Blue-Jay did not know.

He gripped the parcel. "What did Ian Cameron do to the sister of Rosalyn Pryce? She said she would never forgive him for whatever it was."

John put a hand to his arm, the touch warm. "I wish there was time to tell you. I truly do. Maybe Thomas will tell it. But I'd ask one thing more of you, should you continue to Shiloh. Show Ian the grace you would desire, should anyone hold a wrong against *you*."

Blue-Jay made no promise as he tossed his rifle into the wagon bed and hoisted himself in after. He sat with his back against a barrel, his father's shoulder pressed close. Thomas clasped John Reynold's hand, then headed for the wagon's driving bench, into which he vaulted with the lithe grace of the young.

From the hidden place below them came the girl's muffled voice. "Thank you, Mister John. Pray for us."

John stood near the wagon. "Always," he said to their hidden cargo. "God speed you on your journey, Esther. You will have my prayers, and Cecily's, until I hear of your safe arrival. All of you shall."

Thomas snapped the lines. The wagon lurched forward, leaving John standing in the road.

Suddenly the man trotted after them. Blue-Jay scrambled to the rear of the wagon, just as John reached it and said, "If ever you're in need, open that letter and use what you find there. Ian won't begrudge it. But until that moment, guard it well."

"I will." The answer had slipped out, more reflex than agreement. But it was said.

John Reynold halted. The wagon rolled on. The space between widened until darkness swallowed Blue-Jay's last sight of the man.

McCOMB PUBLIC LIBRARY
McCOMB, OHIO

7

Anisguti — Planting Moon (May)

They had traveled toward the Yadkin River until night began to gray with morning's approach, seeing nothing of Edmund MacKinnon along the road. Either he had also ridden through the night, or they had missed his camp.

"Or he did not go this way at all," Runs-Far surmised, apparently unbothered. "Perhaps some business took him elsewhere."

Blue-Jay knew not what to think. He needed sleep, something he had got little of in the wagon's jolting bed.

Concealed from the road by a thicket of rhododendron, sheltered by a mixed grove of pines and oak trees, they made a fireless camp. What of their provisions could be eaten cold—jerked venison, wheaten bread and cheese, dried berries—they ate, then settled in to wait for darkness again, hoping no pursuit yet mustered.

Haggard after the night's travel, Thomas appeared wary but unafraid. The girl flinched at every rustle in the brush concealing them. The damp air was warming with the sun's rising, but Esther huddled into herself, shoulders hunched beneath a plain-woven coat of thin wool. It might once have been black but was faded now to a muddy gray, worn threadbare in spots and too big for the girl.

She was glad to be out from that space in the wagon's bed, though Thomas had told Blue-Jay how to remove the board directly above her so she could at least sit up, braced against the wagon's lurching, with Blue-Jay ready to conceal her again should they pass anyone in the night.

Now Blue-Jay got his first good look at her in daylight. Though more accustomed to the beauty of his own people, he thought hers a comely face, smooth and richly brown. But would anyone take her for a boy? Maybe, if she kept that shapeless hat on, covering her kerchief-wrapped hair, which she had refused to let Cecily Reynold shave to complete the ruse.

The girl ate in silence, watching Blue-Jay and Runs-Far sidelong. When finished she stood, hesitated, then seemed to gather courage to venture through the trees down to the creek.

"Don't go far," Thomas cautioned as she passed him taking the horses from their traces.

"Just doing the necessary." She slipped from sight among a straggle of brush lining the creek's bank.

She was back moments later, something cradled in her hands. As she neared, Blue-Jay saw it was a turtle's shell, its top nearly black, edged with small red markings, its bottom yellow. It was not much bigger than the girl's hand. She hovered by the wagon, standing back from where Blue-Jay and his father sat finishing their food. She jumped when Thomas came up behind her.

"I don't reckon they bite."

The girl ducked her head, hat brim hiding her face, but she sat down near Runs-Far with the turtle shell in her lap. It was a pretty thing, undamaged though empty and dried.

Runs-Far leaned closer. "You found that along the creek?"

The girl's dark eyes flicked at him then down at a patch of clover growing beside her knee. She picked a stem, studied its leaves. "Uh-huh."

"See those small red markings? It is the shell of the painted turtle. May I hold it?"

The girl handed it over to Blue-Jay's father, who held the shell between cupped hands large enough to encompass it. "The creature who made its home here has gone away. Do you wish to keep its shell?"

The girl twirled her clover stem. "Don't reckon I could set up home in it."

Runs-Far's laugh was soft. "Do you object to me keeping it?"

"It's just an old shell. Keep it if you want."

"S'gi. Thank you." The girl went back to picking at the clover. Runs-Far's gray brows flickered as he regarded her. "It will not be for you as it was for the creature that once lived in this shell."

A frown pinched the skin between Esther's eyes. "What's that mean?"

"You have left behind a place, but there will be another for you. Someplace better, I think."

The girl spoke in a whisper. "I hope so."

Blue-Jay glanced between them. What did his father want with the turtle shell? Maybe he had asked for it just to have something to say to the girl. Blue-Jay was trying to think of how to add to the conversation when she spoke again, gaze fastened on her fingers rooting through the clover.

"Miss Cecily told me about you two. That you'd be coming along, not to be a'feared of you." Her gaze flicked up again, traveling over their garments, their faces. "Is you both Indians? Or just the one of you?"

"We are both what you would call Cherokees," Runs-Far replied. "Runs-Far is my name. This one, Blue-Jay, has been my son almost since the day his mother birthed him. But I was not the man who put him in her belly."

"A white man did that." Thomas had returned from hobbling the team. He settled beside Esther, who fixed Blue-Jay with a quizzical gaze.

"Was your mama white too?"

Blue-Jay did not wish to speak of himself. Runs-Far held no such compunction. "His mother was white, Cherokee, African. All of them in part. She was born a slave. Like you she left her place of bondage. She found her own people. Her Bird Clan people of the Tsalagi. She was taken from us when this one was twelve summers." He bent a nod at Blue-Jay. "Taken by soldiers and sold to the mistress of Mountain Laurel. There she birthed our last child. The daughter I have never seen. This we have learned."

"Must've been ages ago." Esther's gaze lifted toward Runs-Far's white hair. Then she drew breath. "Wait. By *mistress* you don't mean Lucinda Cameron, but that other one that died afore I was born? Master Hugh's first wife?"

"That's right," Thomas said. "This is Lily's father and brother."

Esther gaped. "Does Lily know about you? Does Seona?"

Thomas gave her arm a playful poke. "You know they don't. It was always a question, where Lily's mama came from—other than she was snatched from the Cherokee."

"I mind it." The girl scrunched her brows at Blue-Jay and his father. "What took you so long to come looking?"

Blue-Jay wished Thomas and the girl would sleep. Then he could speak to his father about when they would part company with these two.

"That is a long story," Runs-Far said. "Maybe during our travels tomorrow I will tell it to you. But there is a story *I* would hear told. My son was getting you away from that other place when I read the letter from my granddaughter, Seona, then spoke with John Reynold about her. Blue-Jay does not know what happened between my granddaughter and the one called Ian Cameron. Some of it I know, but I would ask one of you to tell that story. You both were part of it, yes?"

Of all the things Blue-Jay wished to hear no more about, Ian Cameron was uppermost. But Thomas was already telling the story of how his father and the father of Ian Cameron met in battle during the colonies' war with the British, how they became friends and had a business together in Boston after that war. A business of making books. Thomas and Ian Cameron had been as close as brothers once. Then Hugh Cameron, Ian's uncle, had asked his nephew to come to North Carolina to be his heir, the next master of Mountain Laurel. There Ian had grown besotted with—

"Fell in *love* with," Esther corrected.

—Seona, enslaved to the young man's uncle, as was her mother, Lily. Thomas had come south with Ian, but with his own purpose in mind, that of helping any slaves he could to the freedom he had grown to manhood enjoying, while pretending to be Ian's slave. Thomas had learned Ian meant to see Seona freed, then marry her.

"That's when I let Seona know *my* plan. I gave her the choice of letting me help her to freedom—without marriage to Ian thrown in. I still don't know whether she might have chosen my way, though I reckon not. But all plans got thwarted by Hugh Cameron's wife, Lucinda, and his overseer, who caught me and Seona in the night while Ian was away, sold us on Lucinda's orders, then made Ian believe we'd run away together."

Esther interrupted again. "Then Mister Ian got clawed up by a painter-cat, out trying to track 'em down. Only there weren't no trail to follow. It was all a ruse thought up by that wicked Miss Lucinda, who wanted Ian to marry one of her daughters so Mountain Laurel would stay with her blood. Once Mister Ian got over being clawed up and fevered, so much time had passed I reckon he gave up on Seona, 'cause he decided to stay and be Master Hugh's heir anyway—and up and married Miss Judith, his younger stepdaughter. She was the nice one. Thomas wasn't there when all that fell out. Mister Ian hadn't found him yet either."

Blue-Jay recalled Rosalyn Pryce's chilling words. *I have not forgiven him for breaking my sister's heart.* "Judith is the sister of the one we saw last night?"

"She is. Was." Thomas appeared ready to cut the story short in favor of sleep. "It was months before Ian learned the truth and tracked both me and Seona down, brought us back to Mountain Laurel—me sick with the swamp fever, Seona carrying his child."

"But he'd married Miss Judith, thinking Seona weren't never coming back." Esther gave a shrug, edging the coat collar up around her ears. "He still loved Seona and hadn't known about the baby coming, until too late. Those were sorry days."

"That they were." Thomas rubbed at his eyes then rose, meeting Blue-Jay's lifted gaze. "I'm tired to the bone. Keep watch, will you? Wake me when you need to sleep."

Blue-Jay nodded. It was time he unrolled his father's blanket so Runs-Far could sleep. But his father was not done talking.

"Is there more to say of my granddaughter, after she returned to Mountain Laurel?"

"A little." Esther glanced at Thomas, gone to lie in the wagon's shade, hat over his face. "Seona's boy, Gabriel—guess he'd be about four now—was born on a hot summer day down by the creek. In a thunderstorm! Mister Ian midwifed his own son, underneath a big ol' willow tree. Lily ran down to help when we heard. They brought Seona and the baby up to the cabins. Then... things went on. Miss Rosalyn had married Mister Gideon and gone to Chesterfield. Miss Judith was carrying a baby of her own. No one knew what to do about Seona and Gabriel. I don't think Mister Ian could bring himself to free them by that point, 'cause right after he did it they'd have had to leave North Carolina. Autumn come around. Mister Ian and Miss Judith's baby girl, Mandy, got born. But that very day the Big House caught fire and Master Hugh died. Then everything changed again."

Esther's mouth trembled. "My mama and daddy... they belonged to Miss Lucinda, from her first marriage. Me too. She left Mountain Laurel that night, taking us all to Miss Rosalyn at Chesterfield. Soon after, we heard Lily, Seona, and Gabriel finally went north to live with Mister Ian's mama and daddy in Boston—turned out Master Hugh had freed them without telling nobody, weeks afore he died.

"Later, when Miss Judith passed, having herself another baby that come too soon, I got to go back to Mountain Laurel with Miss Lucinda and see them that was left—Mister Ian and Mandy. Our cook, Naomi, like a second mama to me. Her old daddy, Malcolm, who talked like he come from Scotland though he didn't. And Naomi's growed-up son, Ally—biggest man I ever laid eyes on, kindest too, but simple in the head, like a child."

Tears filled the girl's eyes and spilled. "Anyway... next I knew, we hear tell Mister Ian done sold Mountain Laurel and took 'em all away!"

Thomas stirred on his blanket with a grunt.

Esther slapped a hand over her mouth. "I can't talk no more about it," she mumbled around fingers threaded with tears.

Runs-Far put a hand on her shoulder and gave a gentle squeeze. "You have suffered much loss, including your parents, so the wife of John Reynold told me. That is hard. But you are on the path to being with those others you named—Naomi, Malcolm, Ally. Those ones long missed, yes?"

The girl wiped at her tears. "Thomas says they went with Ian to New York. To Shiloh. All I want now in this life—if I can't have my daddy—is to see them again."

Runs-Far nodded. "Creator-Jesus sees them, and you, and your father as well. He knows the path you take. He will guide. But now you need sleep. So do I," he added with the reassuring smile Blue-Jay recalled as a boy come to him with some upset only a father could put right. A father who knew how to pray, to draw hope and comfort from Creator, and give it to others.

While Runs-Far helped the girl spread a blanket under the wagon, Blue-Jay sat turning over his father's words, moved by the girl's plight. He had heard of Esther's losses from the mouth of Rosalyn Pryce but had been too worried for himself in that moment to fully comprehend them. Her mother was dead, her father sold far away—as good as dead to her. The girl was barely older than he had been when his mother was taken, but he had been left with a father. A sister. A clan who cared for him.

Esther wiggled out of her coat, folded it to cushion her head, took off the drooping hat, and lay down. Runs-Far returned to the fire with their blankets and knelt, plucking up stones and acorns that would press into old backs, tossing them into the brush.

His father had spoken confidently of Creator-Jesus and the finding of paths. Blue-Jay wished he felt such certainty. For years he had believed he could have saved his mother if he had been less selfish. Perhaps all he would have gained was a few more moons with her before his sister's birth killed her, but he would have known himself a better son. And what of that sister? Would he have resented her had she been born in their village, had he watched her grow and thrive? Blamed her instead?

He could not force such ugly words off his tongue.

"Edo'da, why do you think the girl wishes to go to that one who once enslaved her, that Ian Cameron?"

His father grew still, cradling a handful of acorns. "That man did not enslave her. You heard what she said. She was the slave of Lucinda Cameron. The one who caused much pain with her deceit."

"Still I do not think this Ian Cameron can be a good man." Blue-Jay shook his head, hearing again the voice of John Reynold at their parting, talking of *grace.* Why would a man need grace unless he had done a thing deserving of judgement?

I have not forgiven him for breaking my sister's heart. Had he also broken the heart of Chickadee's daughter?

His father had stopped tidying the ground. He lay down on his blanket, tiredness in the lines bracketing his eyes and mouth. "We do not know enough of Ian Cameron to say what sort of man he is. No doubt he is as all men walking this earth. A sinner—one covered in the blood of Creator-Jesus, we may hope."

Blue-Jay regretted mentioning the man. He did not wish to talk of him or anything else to do with Camerons, Mountain Laurel, or sisters. "Sleep, Edo'da. When the river we follow turns westward, we will part from these ones, let them go their way. We will go ours. We will go home."

Runs-Far turned over on his blanket. "We will see."

It was getting on toward morning, the third night traveling along the Yadkin River, when Blue-Jay heard the horses coming on the road behind them. Though not the first time it had happened, Blue-Jay's shoulders stiffened beneath Thomas's coat, which he wore along with breeches and a shirt tied at the throat with a strip of matching cloth, like a white man.

He had worn them since the previous night when they passed a man on horseback who stopped them. That man had found it strange, Thomas doing the driving while Blue-Jay sat in the wagon bed beside his father, atop the board under which Esther hid. Taking him for a white man, he had addressed Blue-Jay, who tried to answer as a white man would while his heart pounded, afraid for his father and the hidden girl.

Though the man had not asked about runaway slaves before going his way, Thomas soon halted the wagon, gave over his coat, and found the garments that fit Blue-Jay well enough to pass in the dark as his own. Blue-Jay had donned Thomas's hat then taken over driving the team, leaving his father and Thomas in the bed, ready to hide the girl again at need. There had been none until now, past a village where the rattle of the wagon had alarmed a dog into barking.

Blue-Jay glanced back. Only a gray stripe on the horizon marked the coming day, but his eyes were accustomed to the dark. There were two horsemen, coming up fast.

"Steady," Thomas said above the wagon's rattle. "Drive like you've every right to be on this road."

The words were barely out before one rider called ahead. "Halt that wagon!"

Crouched behind the driving bench, Thomas groaned. "I can't be seen."

The lines bit into Blue-Jay's clenched fingers. "Why can you not?"

"No time. Pull over!"

Forest hemmed both sides of the narrow road beyond the village. Blue-Jay obeyed the urgency in Thomas's voice, edging the team toward the thickest shadows. Before the wagon rolled to a halt Thomas vaulted over its side and slipped into the trees. Neither rider gave a shout, as if they had not seen. Blue-Jay heard his father murmuring. Praying? Reassuring the girl?

Pray for me, Edo'da.

The riders were upon them. One moved his horse to stand across their path. The other—Blue-Jay had the impression in the coming dawn of a man well-dressed in the way of the unega—edged his tall horse close to the wagon, peering at Blue-Jay, then at his father, seated among the barrels and crates in the bed, still wearing breechclout and leggings under his shirt.

"An Indian," the man said in surprise. "Yours?"

Blue-Jay's mouth had dried. He fought the urge to slap the lines across the horses' backs and let them bolt. That would do no good. He must brazen this out.

"He is mine. Is that what you stop us to ask?"

The man's gaze sharpened on him. Blue-Jay had not sounded like Edmund MacKinnon, or Charlie Spencer, or any man who called this land east of the mountains home, though he had tried.

"We're hunting a runaway. A girl. Skinny thing. Middling brown of complexion. She's wearing a calico headscarf and a striped petticoat, a blue short-gown. My wife, whose personal maid she is, assures me she took no other garments with her when she ran. Have you seen such a girl on the road?"

Blue-Jay realized two things in that terrible moment. This was Chesterfield's master. And Rosalyn Pryce had done more than keep her silence. Aside from that calico head-wrapping worn under the hat, Esther had run away wearing boy's garments. "I have not seen such a one," he said, silently thanking that unhappy woman for giving him the means to walk the fine line of truth, even as his heart lodged in his throat, beating hard.

Darkness was lifting. The trees lining the road had taken distinct shape. So had the features of the man on the tall horse. He had a dark sweep of brows above deep-set eyes that bore hard into whatever they fixed upon. Just now that was something in the wagon's bed.

"What is that? You—hand it to me."

Blue-Jay turned as Runs-Far crawled across the wagon to what the man indicated—Esther's head-wrapping. Fear lanced deep into his belly as he remembered. Yesterday had been warm. The girl had complained of her scalp sweating under both wrapping and hat. She had removed the wrapping, patterned in faded reds and greens. Runs-Far gave it to the man.

"Where did you get this?"

"It was lying on the road," Blue-Jay said. Again, it was no lie. The girl had dropped it over the wagon's side by accident. Thomas had leapt out to retrieve it.

The man's eyes narrowed. "When? Where?"

"Yesterday. A long way back. I do not recall exactly."

The man whose horse stood across their path spoke. "It hers, Mr. Pryce?"

"It is. I've seen her wear it."

"Keep it," Blue-Jay said, knowing not what else to add.

The man tucked the head-wrapping into his coat. It was light enough now Blue-Jay could discern the color of his eyes. A flat murky green, showing no hint of human kindness. Blue-Jay suppressed a shudder.

"We're on the right road. She cannot be far." The man's horse side-stepped. He circled it to face Blue-Jay again, who licked his lips and swallowed. "If you see the girl, detain her. She belongs to me, Gideon Pryce, of Chesterfield Plantation, back in Randolph County. You'll be rewarded for your trouble."

The two men heeled their horses on down the road, leaving Blue-Jay with hands trembling around the lines, waiting on the roadside while dawn swept over them. He startled when his father spoke, as if to himself.

"They have ridden on. It is all right."

Blue-Jay did not contradict his father but felt no such reassurance. They needed to get off that road before someone else came along. In moments Thomas showed himself and they drove on, seeking a place to hide for the day. No one spoke until the wagon was parked down an overgrown lane, behind an empty cabin half fallen in on itself. There was little hope of finding food growing in the abandoned garden behind the cabin, still Esther, shaken from her near discovery, dug around in case a carrot or potato had been overlooked since last harvest—whenever that had been.

"Sorry to leave you to face that," Thomas said while he and Blue-Jay unhitched the team. "Pryce knows my face. I did some coopering for him while posing as Ian's slave. It would have been over for us all had he spotted me."

"It is good you did what you did," Runs-Far said, holding to the horses' bridles.

"It showed me what your son is capable of." Thomas was gazing at Blue-Jay. "We best make full use of it. We need to take another road—Pryce will be watching this one—and we need to travel faster. Only way to do that is by day, at least until we're into Virginia."

"We are not going to Virginia. We will go our way westward. Today."

Thomas looked ready to argue, but the girl spoke first, having come up behind them in time to hear Blue-Jay's words. "You leaving us?"

Blue-Jay turned to see her there, a dirty carrot dangling from one hand.

"I thought you was going with us all the way to Shiloh." Dismay made Esther's voice shrill. "What about Lily? Seona? Don't you want to find them? What about *me*? Mister Gideon would be dragging me back to Chesterfield, weren't for you two."

Blue-Jay's father released the horses and moved to stand next to the girl. "Daughter, do not fear. We are not leaving you."

"Edo'da ... we must."

Runs-Far ignored Blue-Jay. "Tell us of this other road," he said to Thomas. "And what you are thinking about it. You have a plan, I think."

"A bit of one." Thomas rubbed his stubbled chin, glancing between them. "There's a road running northeast from here. We passed it south of that village. Just across the Carolina border there's a family that helped me once. We'd make it before nightfall if we travel through the day. But we need you for that—unless we leave the wagon and proceed afoot. Reckon you can take the horses. I'll find a way to repay Reynold."

"You mean we got to *walk* to New York?" Esther all but squeaked. "How far is that?"

Runs-Far shook his head. "Too far."

Fear cut a path through Blue-Jay's mind. For himself, his father, and the girl. He did not want her falling into Gideon Pryce's hands. He had not liked what he saw in that man's eyes. "Is it going to make you safe, getting across into Virginia?"

Thomas hesitated. "Pryce or his slave catchers could follow us anywhere. The law gives him that right. The danger won't end at the state line, but at least we could hole up awhile—and your white face can get us safe that far."

Blue-Jay wanted no part of this undertaking, but there was the girl and her pleading eyes. There was Thomas, risking his life to make hers a life worth living. And there was his father, seeming dispossessed of any regard for his own wellbeing, asking Thomas, "It is not far into Virginia, this farm and these good people?"

"Four, maybe five miles over the line. They're Quakers."

They knew of Quakers, a people who had different ideas than most unega about things like slavery. And Indians.

Runs-Far said, "This is not so far out of the way you wish to go, my son."

Perhaps if Blue-Jay had refused to look again at Esther he might have found it in him to refuse a final time. But he looked—and saw himself as a boy, pleading with his father to keep looking for his mother, never admitting he believed he was to blame for the loss of her. His father had not headed those pleas. Blue-Jay's guilt had become entrenched. Did he want this girl to remember him as the man who would not help her?

"All right. I will drive the wagon to these Quakers. But that is as far as I will go, Edo'da. Do not ask me to go one step farther."

8

SOUTHERN VIRGINIA

Something was wrong. This was clear the moment the wagon rattled to a halt in the cabin yard and the man came out to stand on the narrow porch, gripping a rifle aimed at them, a thing Blue-Jay thought a Quaker would never do. As the man narrowed his blue eyes and pursed his thin lips, Blue-Jay scrambled to remember all Thomas had told him he must say to the people of this place to find the welcome they hoped for. And the aid.

Before he could say anything, the man shot a look at Runs-Far, sitting atop the boards that hid not just Esther, but Thomas too. The man's eyes hardened above bristled cheeks. "Who are you?"

It was a thing no one had thought to discuss, what Blue-Jay was to call himself if asked. He all but shouted the first name that came to mind. "Pauling! That is the name I claim."

"Pauling? You talk funny. Ain't from around here?"

"No. From over the mountains. Tennessee."

The answer did not banish the man's suspicion. "Ain't got connections Overmountain. Don't know no Paulings. What's your business with me?"

"I have for you . . ." What were the words he was meant to use? "Jars—of clay. Two jars. Can you take them?"

"Jars?" The man's mouth bowed downward. "For what?"

A thumping came from the wagon bed. Blue-Jay peered over his shoulder at his father. Runs-Far's hands were clenched on the blanket wrapping his shoulders. His feet were still. The thumping came again. This time Blue-Jay knew who made it—knew it for a signal to abandon the notion of finding help in that place.

"Sorry to disturb." He tugged the hat's brim, as Thomas had showed him to do. It was a way of being polite. In his eagerness to get away, he nearly pulled the hat down over his face. Righting it, he added, "Good day to you."

The man who was no Quaker shouted ugly English words until they were well away from his cabin.

Had they come to the wrong place? Blue-Jay could not think straight enough to know what to do. Back out on the road they had traveled to reach that farm, he turned the team northward, deeper into Virginia, while behind him in the wagon bed his father took up the board from over Thomas and Esther, so they could speak. Blue-Jay did not catch his father's words, or anything from Thomas, but heard Esther plain: "He talking, but ain't making a lick of sense!"

Blue-Jay called back, "What more is wrong?"

"Stop the wagon, my son. There is a problem."

The problem was Thomas, sweating in the space under the wagon's false bottom. It took all three to get him out of it to lie in the bed where at least he could breathe. The skin of his face was hot to the touch. His breath came shallow.

"Swamp fever. Felt it coming on when I woke ..."

"He gets like this sometimes," Esther explained. "Since he got sold away by Miss Lucinda and wound up working in a swamp back east."

Blue-Jay scanned the road. Empty. For now. "What is to be done for him?"

"Reverend Pauling had this sickness," Runs-Far said. "It will leave him, for a time anyway, if we can get him good medicine."

"Jesuit bark . . . in my bag." Thomas closed his eyes. "Steep a tea. Nasty stuff . . . and I'm nigh out."

"I will need to heat water," Runs-Far said. "We must find a safe place."

Blue-Jay scanned the road ahead where it dipped into a stretch of forest. It would not be a long stretch. Not if what lay ahead was like the last miles had been. Thickly settled, farm after farm. Few wild places between.

Thomas squinted at Blue-Jay with fever-dulled eyes. "Pauling? That the name I heard you use?"

"Never mind names," Esther said. "What we gonna do?"

Blue-Jay drew a steadying breath, regretting he had ever agreed to ride in this wagon, even one night. But if he abandoned these two now, he might as well find that Gideon Pryce and hand Esther straight over. That he would not do.

"I am going to pull into those trees ahead." He took up the lines and smacked the horses' rumps. "Be watchful as I do so. Pray no one sees."

Runs-Far made the medicine tea then smothered their fire. Thomas drank it, grimacing, in the rough camp pitched in a declivity that hid them by the banks of a tiny stream. Blue-Jay and Runs-Far knelt beside the sick man and questioned him.

Would he recover now that he had had some of the bark tea?

"Not with one dose . . ."

Where could they get more of this fever-bark? And where could they go from that place to find safety?

The next safe place Thomas knew of was in a town called Staunton, days to the north. Esther sat at Thomas's head with a rag wet from the stream. He reached for her hand, visibly afraid for the first time Blue-Jay had seen.

Runs-Far spoke. "Cade and Jeremiah Ring were on their way to a place in Virginia, on the James River. Long Meadows, they called it. If they are still there, they would help us." He placed a hand on Thomas's chest. "Is that near?"

Thomas shut his eyes. "Nearer than Staunton, maybe. James is a mighty long river."

"I do not recall where on the river this Long Meadows is found," Runs-Far admitted.

"Who's Cade and that other you named?" Esther asked, hopeful. "Friends of yours?"

While his father told of Cade and Jeremiah Ring, Blue-Jay held his peace. He did not want to speak of Long Meadows, or what he recalled about that place. He had agreed to get Thomas and Esther to the Quakers. Though it turned out there were no Quakers—Thomas surmised they had sold that farm since he had last been there—Blue-Jay did not want to go any farther north.

Perhaps he did not have to.

"There is a letter," he said, snatching everyone's attention. "It is addressed to Ian Cameron, but John Reynold said we may open it at need, use what we find there."

They stared, waiting for him to go on. Finally Esther asked, "What's in a letter can help?"

Blue-Jay went to the wagon and found the parcel handed to him in darkness, tucked into his bag where he had put it that first night. With his knife he cut its bindings and found inside a letter sealed with wax. This he put aside in favor of a folded leather scrap. He brought it to the others, kneeling so all could see. With it resting on his palm, he unfolded the leather to reveal... yellow pebbles. A dozen, maybe twenty. Most no bigger than the seeds of sunflowers.

Thomas eyed Blue-Jay in some surprise. "I know what it is. Reynold let me in on the secret. Reckon it's fine to tell you."

Esther's disappointment was plain. "What good's shiny rocks gonna do us? And what secret?"

"Not rocks . . . *gold*."

Esther drew her head back. "Like money?"

"Exactly like."

Blue-Jay, Runs-Far, and the girl peered again at what the leather scrap contained. Esther asked what Blue-Jay figured all were thinking. "Where's it from?"

Thomas's mouth curled at its corners. "Up on the ridge . . . along the creek that once divided Reynold's land from Mountain Laurel."

Esther's eyebrows shot up under her hat's brim. "I know that creek. Why ain't I ever seen gold in it?"

Blue-Jay interrupted with a more pertinent question. "Can this gold be traded for the medicine you need?"

"Not by the likes of us."

"Who then?"

"A planter could make use of it without raising too much question." Thomas winced as he swallowed. "Long Meadows . . . that a plantation?"

Runs-Far nodded. "Cade called it so. If he is there, he will let no harm come to either of you. He is a good man, once a slave himself but now counted a son of that place. If we can find it."

"How?" Esther raised helpless hands. "We ain't got enough to go on."

No one spoke in answer to that, though Blue-Jay knew he could. And saw that he must do so.

"Long Meadows is near a place called Lynchburg. The master is Ambrose Kincaid." With a sigh of resignation, he met Thomas's fevered gaze. "Is that enough to go on?"

Lynchburg took four more tedious nights of travel to reach. Thomas rode in the open bed so Runs-Far could tend him, as did Esther. "To keep my bones from being rattled apart," she said more than once. But they were not stopped again by Gideon Pryce or any other slave-catchers.

Finding Lynchburg proved the easiest part. To find Long Meadows, Blue-Jay was forced to inquire in the yards of three different taverns where sleepy maids and stablemen were at work in the damp dark of early morning. Following directions given at the last tavern, they came to Long Meadows in the pre-dawn gray, approaching from a track that paralleled a wider lane running straight through fields newly planted. It led to the main house, which was made of red brick with white columns, larger than any structure Blue-Jay or Runs-Far had ever seen.

The track they followed took them off to the side of that house, past rows of white buildings Blue-Jay identified as the shops where slaves did their work. He drove the team past, slowing to a crawl because here chickens wandered free. Up ahead a small child darted across the track. It was like driving through a village, all of it belonging to one man inside one big house. The few slaves outside the shops flashed Blue-Jay quick glances, likely taking him for a white man come there on white man's business. Most cast a second look at Runs-Far, visible in the wagon's bed. Thomas lay unconscious. He was no help to Blue-Jay in deciding where in this place he should go, who he should seek. Esther had concealed herself under the wagon boards, warned to keep quiet until—or if—Cade was found.

The lane ended at what Blue-Jay marked the cookhouse by the smells drifting from its open door. People of all shades of brown stood outside the structure to receive the breakfast an old woman doled from a kettle into bowls. That woman paused her ladle, eying the wagon and Blue-Jay.

"Welcome to Long Meadows, sir," she called from the door. "What you come delivering so early? Something for the kitchen, I reckon, seeing as you come this far in. Got breakfast for the house yet to tend but give me a moment and I'll send you out a girl."

She turned, calling to someone inside the cookhouse. A younger woman squeezed out past her and came toward the wagon, brushing floured hands on the apron fronting her long blue skirt. She was darker-skinned than the older woman, broad of feature, her gaze curious, a little wary.

"Morning, sir. What you got for us? Who you needing to speak to about it?"

"Good morning," Blue-Jay said. "I have nothing for your cookhouse."

"Why you here then, may I ask?" Politeness overlay the woman's query, but her eyes widened as she took in the wagon bed. "That an Indian grandpa with you?"

One of the men at the cookhouse, well-muscled and tall, left the waiting group and came to stand beside the woman. "Everything all right, Annie?"

The woman, Annie, planted her hands on her hips. "Don't know. Mister here say he ain't delivering nothing. Maybe he here to fetch something away?"

The big man's gaze took in Blue-Jay, then Runs-Far, then the wagon itself with narrowed eyes, giving the impression he saw more than did Annie. "What can we be doing for you, sir?"

"I hope to find here one called Cade," Blue-Jay said.

Surprise marked the man's features. "You know Cade?"

"We journeyed for a while with him and his brother, Jeremiah Ring, on their way to you here. He will know us. He will help."

"Help with what?" Annie asked.

The man had stepped up to peer inside the wagon. Frowning, he glanced at Blue-Jay, still perched on the driving bench. "That your man laid out here? Looking poorly, he be."

Annie stood on her toes to peer inside the wagon's bed and gasped at sight of Thomas. "What you want with Cade, though? Begging your pardon but he ain't no physic."

"Whatever you wanted from him," the man said, "Cade's done been here and gone, Mister Jeremiah with him. They cut their visit short."

"I'll run fetch Master Ambrose. You wait right here." Before Blue-Jay could stop her, Annie was headed for the house at a trot, skirt hiked above dewy grass.

Most of the people—slaves, Blue-Jay guessed—were going about their business. The big man stayed.

"I ain't meaning you to speak of what you ain't of a mind to tell, but I've noted something about this wagon. Its bed be a might shallow—to judge by the height of its sides." Dark eyes, shrewd with intelligence, traveled over the conveyance. "I'm head carpenter here at Long Meadows, nigh on twenty years. Such things jump out at me, things others maybe overlook. I'm guessing this sick man ain't the only one you two is seeking help for?"

"That is a good guess," Runs-Far said, speaking for the first time. "Maybe you will help with that, after we have seen to the sick one here?"

Blue-Jay observed the silent understanding that passed between his father and the carpenter. Then another voice called out, the words indistinct. From the house a tall white man was coming with long strides. The man wore a dark green coat and matching breeches, buckled shoes and fine white stockings, but his head was uncovered. His hair, cropped and brushed forward toward his brow, caught the sunrise in a coppery blaze.

Ambrose Kincaid—it could be no other—came straight to the wagon and peered in at Thomas, who was slit-eyed and breathing loud, unaware of those around him. Then the master of Long Meadows took in Runs-Far, who could be nothing other than what he was, an elderly Indian. Blue-Jay presented a more puzzling picture as he alighted from the bench and stood among these strangers.

"These men are yours?" Ambrose Kincaid asked.

"They are mine, but neither is my property." Blue-Jay met the man's gaze straight on, seeing nothing of the cruelty he had glimpsed in the eyes of Gideon Pryce. There was authority. Was there also kindness? "I am Blue-Jay. Born to the Bird Clan of the Tsalagi. This is my father, Runs-Far. We are on a journey, he and I. As for this one you see lying sick with fever, he is called Thomas Ross. He is a free man. We seek help for him and have the means to pay for it."

Ambrose Kincaid had followed this speech with his red eyebrows rising higher and higher, pushing his high forehead into wrinkles. Without hesitation he cut to what Blue-Jay thought would be the heart of the matter for such a man.

"What means of payment?"

"If you are willing to help, we will show you that means."

"You will excuse me if I don't take the word of strangers that trespass on my lands asking aid for a man likely to be—"

"Cousin?" a voice called, a woman's voice that turned Blue-Jay's head in startled recognition, and relief. It was the wife of Cade's nephew, Jesse. Tamsen Kincaid. She was heading straight for them, draped in what seemed a vast amount of gold-hued cloth and moving with the awkward gait of a woman now great with child, flanked by her young daughters and the woman from the cookhouse, Annie.

Tamsen stopped short when she took in his face and Runs-Far sitting in the wagon. "You two?" She approached then as quickly as her burdened body could bring her. "I never thought to see you both again. Certainly not here."

"Tamsen, you oughtn't to be out." Ambrose Kincaid aimed a frown at Annie, as if he held her at fault for this circumstance. "Or on your feet, for that matter, so near your time."

"Don't scowl at Annie," Tamsen said, reproving the man without heat. "As for being on my feet, my goodness, Cousin, this isn't my first time. Besides, I'm reassured by the midwife as well as your physician that all is well. I saw you leave the house and inquired what was afoot. And a good thing," she added, peering into the wagon's bed and spying Thomas.

"How is it you know these men?" Ambrose asked.

"They're Cade's friends. Both were recent guests in my home. I'd be much obliged if you would receive them into yours now. And permit this one with them the care he needs."

Before Long Meadow's master could agree or object, the very pregnant wife of Jesse Kincaid—who had obviously decided to journey to this place to bear her child, after all—had taken charge of matters. While the carpenter helped Runs-Far from the wagon, more men were called from nearby shops to carry Thomas to the house, leaving Esther concealed inside the wagon's false bottom.

Blue-Jay lingered long enough to catch the gaze of the carpenter, who nodded and said low-voiced, "We know what you carry. We'll tend it for you while you're here."

9

LONG MEADOWS PLANTATION, VIRGINIA

The big house bustled with the comings and goings of a physician, a midwife, and each one's servant. Long Meadows slaves passed outside the room where Thomas lay, recovering from his fever. Their attention had shifted from him to Tamsen Kincaid once her baby started coming in the dark of that morning.

It was getting on to midday when Blue-Jay, on his way to Thomas's room near the top of the ornate stairs leading up from the main rooms of the house, stood aside to let a housemaid bearing a stack of cloths hurry pass. Blue-Jay had never been under the same roof as a woman giving birth. Hearing the proceedings as the door to that room opened and shut to admit the housemaid, he winced, and prayed it would not last much longer.

Jesse Kincaid had brought his wife and daughters down the mountains to their Cousin Ambrose, then left again with Cade and Jeremiah Ring a day before Blue-Jay drove the wagon up to the cookhouse. Jesse had meant to return to Long Meadows before the baby came, but that was happening now. Half a moon earlier than expected, Blue-Jay had heard someone say.

He paused in the doorway of Thomas's room, a small one with walls painted green, containing no more than a bed, a table and washstand, and some chairs for sitting. He had thought to find his father there, where Runs-Far often spent his days since

Thomas had been well enough to talk, but Thomas was alone. On the table by a window lay the turtle shell Esther had found back in North Carolina. It was clear now what his father was doing with it—making himself a rattle. He had whittled a length of maple for a handle, thrust it into the empty shell, then sealed up the edges of the shell with rawhide and sinew. A small hole had been left open for the pile of pebbles on the table. Tufts of fur lay beside it like sleeping mice, ready to adorn the handle.

Thomas was awake in the bed where he had lain for many days. Blue-Jay was restless, wanting to start for home, but his father refused to discuss leaving Long Meadows until Thomas was strong enough to continue his journey with Esther. In all that time those who worked in the cookhouse, shops, and fields of that place had kept the girl concealed from those dwelling in the house. Except for Tamsen. Blue-Jay was unsure how she learned of Esther, but she had told them not to worry for the girl's safety. She would keep her presence a secret from Ambrose Kincaid in case anyone came seeking a runaway matching Esther's description.

"Would he give her to them?" Blue-Jay had asked.

"I'm not sure even Ambrose could answer that," Tamsen said.

Long Meadows' master, it turned out, loved a woman who was one of those Quakers. The woman refused to marry a man who owned slaves, or one outside her kind of people. Even if Ambrose Kincaid turned Quaker, one slave in his possession would be too many for the woman to agree to the match.

"Ambrose tried to join their Meeting, but it seems the slavery issue is a stipulation for their acceptance, as well," Tamsen explained. "It's a lot for him to swallow. It would mean a very different way of life going forward. He's been stewing over the choice for weeks and I honestly don't know what he'll decide. He once idolized Long Meadows. When we first met, it was uppermost of all his conversation. I hope, along with choosing love over riches, he will begin to discover a truer identity in the Almighty."

Despite her hopes, Tamsen thought it unwise to risk Esther's freedom by testing her cousin's resolve prematurely.

Thomas, when the matter was explained, confessed he hoped he had found a new place of refuge for the slaves he intended to keep liberating and guiding to freedom. "I expect Ian, in Shiloh, will prove another. At least for Esther."

Blue-Jay, who had not stopped pondering those words about Ian Cameron, was glad to find Thomas alone now, a book opened on his lap. Thomas looked up from its pages when he darkened the green room's doorway.

"Do you believe Ian Cameron truly loved my sister's daughter?"

Blinking at the abrupt question, Thomas set the book aside. "Come in here, we'll talk about it."

Blue-Jay sat in the chair at the table and waited, staring at the uncompleted rattle.

"Bear in mind, I haven't spoken to Ian in years, though I've had news of him." Thomas, who had not shaved while he had lain abed, ran fingers over the wiry black hairs on his chin. "But Seona went west to Ian when she could have stayed in Boston, she and Lily and Gabriel." He paused, considering Blue-Jay. "What does that tell you?"

"It tells me," said Runs-Far from the doorway, "that we need not worry over Ian Cameron and my granddaughter. But there is something else worrying me now."

Blue-Jay noted a baby's cry, the mewling of a newborn. Or was it... *two* babies? His father answered the unspoken question. "Sons have come. Two born together. They are small, I am told, but both are strong. As you hear."

Still Runs-Far appeared shaken. "Is the mother well?" Blue-Jay asked.

"She is." Runs-Far came to stand at the foot of Thomas's bed. "But men have come. From the top of the stairs I heard them. Gideon Pryce and his man. Ambrose Kincaid has not turned them away."

Blue-Jay stood.

"What's Kincaid done?" Thomas peeled back the bedclothes as if he meant to rise. "He can't know about Esther, can he?"

"I do not know," Runs-Far said. "All I know is he has invited those men into this house to talk, to drink with him, celebrating the mother's good fortune in delivering two healthy sons."

After persuading Thomas he could do no good for Esther by getting out of bed—and much harm if he were seen by Gideon Pryce—Blue-Jay and Runs-Far closed his door and went into an adjoining room, this one with walls painted blue. A large rug lay over the floorboards, worked in reds and golds.

Runs-Far sat in a padded chair beside the door, holding on his lap the tiny moccasins Blue-Jay's mother had made for the daughter she called Chickadee, which Blue-Jay only now noticed his father carried. He held them with his eyes closed, lips moving over prayers. For Esther and Thomas, Blue-Jay was sure. Also for his unknown sister?

Blue-Jay moved to the room's window and gazed out over the cookhouse, past its gardens to the cabins beyond, in one of which the slaves of Long Meadows were hiding Esther. He whispered his own prayers for the girl.

Behind him his father spoke. "Your mother came to The People dressed as a boy, her hair chopped short. In many ways I see her in that girl we brought to this place."

Blue-Jay turned from the window. "Is that why you wish to help her?"

"And because it is a right thing to do." Runs-Far's fingers traced the moccasins' beaded design, but his gaze held Blue-Jay's. "It is time for you to tell me why seeing your mother in that girl makes you want to do the opposite thing."

Blue-Jay's face stung. He would have liked to sit, but there was no second chair in that room. He went on standing, hands fisted. "The girl does make me think of my mother but…" They had fallen into the habit of conversing in English in that place. Blue-Jay shook his head, unable to find the words in that tongue. "Edo'da, I fear that if we make the journey north with these two, if we do not turn for home, something bad will come of it. I will lose you—as I lost my mother. And for the same reason. Because I chose to make a journey with you."

Runs-Far stood and put the moccasins on the chair. He crossed the floor to Blue-Jay. Not as tall as he had once been, he now looked up to meet his son's gaze, the window's light showing clear the strain of their journey—and the distress Blue-Jay's words had wrought. "My son… are you saying you think yourself at fault for the loss of your mother?"

The stone of guilt Blue-Jay had carried for nearly forty winters seemed to expand to the size of that house surrounding them. "I am at fault, Edo'da. You know it."

Runs-Far's hands rose to cup his son's shoulders. His eyes grew moist. "I know no such thing. The thought has never entered my mind. Not once until this moment."

Blue-Jay shut his eyes, disbelieving. "I could have saved her, if I had not insisted on going with you!"

"Or maybe you would have been taken too. I know you do not see yourself as white, but to others you look it. Far more than did your mother. Those soldiers would have taken you away as well."

There was silence in the room, save for Blue-Jay's pounding heart, his labored breathing. From deeper in the house came the babies' crying.

His father said, "Look at me."

Blue-Jay did not want to, but he did. His father's face shone with love. "Each morning since that terrible day we returned to find your mother taken, I have stood with my pipe to pray. I have thanked Creator that you were with me when the soldiers came to our village. Losing your mother wounded me deep. But losing you would have been the end of me. Creator knew it. He allowed you to be with me instead of with your mother and sister that day. That is how I have always seen it."

Blue-Jay searched his father's face, with its broad brow and high cheekbones, the wide mouth, the eyes with their up-tilted corners, the brown skin lined and sagging. How often had he seen this man, a silhouette against a sunrise, the smoke of his pipe going up with his prayers? Never once had he joined his father. He had also prayed alone. Even on this journey. In this place. Like one banished to a distance.

His father held his shoulders still. "Forgive me for not telling you so before this day."

"Of course, Edo'da. You could not have known what I was thinking." Blue-Jay had not known he was crying until he tasted the salt of tears on his tongue.

His father embraced him. They stood there for a time, letting the silence begin to heal the wounds between them. Blue-Jay was thinking of Redwing, knowing this was the need for healing she had seen when she urged him to make this journey, when his father drew back.

"But still you do not wish to make the journey to Shiloh?"

Blue-Jay flinched. It seemed his father had read his mind. "*Hadi.*" No.

Runs-Far released his shoulders and returned to the chair where he had left the moccasins. He picked them up and faced Blue-Jay. "You do not wish to find your sister?"

Blue-Jay debated revealing the ugly thought he had carried since learning of Chickadee—his fear that he would take one look at this sister who had been the death of their mother and would hate her for it.

"What if we find her," he ventured instead, "and she does not wish to know *us*? You know nothing of her."

Runs-Far pressed the moccasins to his heart. "That is another mistaken assumption, my son, but one I am glad you will not have to carry so long. I know much of Chickadee."

Blue-Jay frowned. "What could you know?"

"I know she is a woman as brave as was your mother, for she too has made the journey from slavery to freedom. I know she is a good mother, for she stayed beside her daughter and grandson when she could have gone her own way, made any sort of life she wanted to make. I know she did not let those who have harmed or disappointed her make her heart grow hard, for she has chosen to take a husband—a man of the Mohawk people. I know she is a woman who can forgive, for she did not stop her daughter going to Shiloh to be with a man who once caused them heartache. These things speak to me of her hope, her strength. It is enough to know what sort of woman she is."

A woman who could hold her head high among the daughters of the Aniyunwiya, though she had never known what such an honor should mean. This was how Runs-Far saw his daughter, Chickadee. Seeing her through his father's eyes, Blue-Jay found himself almost convinced she would turn out to be that person.

Almost. But he *did* see one inevitable truth. For good or for ill, he was going to learn if these things about his sister were so, see them with his own eyes. He could deny his father no longer. With a heavy sigh, he reverted to English.

"All right. I will go with you to Shiloh. I will play the part of a white man and drive that wagon. I will help Thomas get the girl safe away from this place and..."

The room's door had been left unlatched. It creaked now as someone out in the passage pushed it open. Blue-Jay no longer heard the crying of babies, nor the bustle that had been going on since the morning. Then the door swung wider to reveal red-haired Ambrose Kincaid, comprehension sharpening his features. He had heard the last of Blue-Jay's words.

Thinking he had just undone their careful hiding of Esther and brought much harm upon the heads of everyone involved, Blue-Jay could not swallow, much less speak.

"Is that one called Pryce there with you?" his father asked with a calm Blue-Jay could not imagine possible.

"He and his confederate have gone." Ambrose's gaze shifted between them. "We shared a drink. I sent them on their way."

Blue-Jay found his voice. "Because you did not know of the girl until now?"

"Not exactly." Ambrose's tone was wry. "I've known Tamsen was hiding something from me. I made it a point not to inquire for details so I wouldn't be forced to choose between speaking falsehood or truth, should a visitation such as I've just entertained occur."

Still it had been a fine line between truth and lie Ambrose Kincaid had walked in the presence of Gideon Pryce, who had shared the details about the runaway he was attempting to locate and return to North Carolina.

"I believe I managed it—like a good Quaker." Ambrose's lips quirked, before his features firmed. "But now I will have the truth about this girl you mentioned. Let's have her out of hiding."

This time there was no one to step in and help. Tamsen was just delivered of two babies, shut up in her room. Thomas was still in his sickbed. There was none but Blue-Jay and Runs-Far to intercede for Esther. But Ambrose Kincaid had sent Gideon Pryce and his man away. With a silent prayer, Blue-Jay cast himself upon the hope of what that action promised.

Leaving Thomas in his bed, none the wiser, the three went out of the house to find Long Meadow's head carpenter, the man who had taken Esther into his care at their arrival. That man took them to the cabin where Esther had hidden all that while.

"Reckon I looked the cornered rabbit, when they all come in," Esther told Thomas when she was allowed in to see him, sitting up in the bed while she perched on its edge. "I hardly even noticed Blue-Jay and his daddy were there, all I could see was that Mister Ambrose staring down at me, arms crossed, brows all scrunched. Then he said, 'I have seen your master, Gideon Pryce. I listened to him speak of you and watched his eyes while he did so, presuming me to be of like mind and heart. I saw in those eyes what my father and grandfather were before me. And the man I have been. The man I shall be no longer.'"

Esther sprang off the bedtick in her relief, while Blue-Jay and Runs-Far tried to stifle their smiles but could not.

"So what happened then?" Thomas asked.

The girl laughed. "Mister Ambrose say he aiming to turn Quaker! So he can marry some woman, I think. But the main thing is, he gonna help us get out of Virginia."

"All of us?" Thomas asked, his gaze not on Esther—still in her boy's clothes though Ambrose had asked his housemaids to find garments more suitable for a young woman to wear—but on Blue-Jay and Runs-Far.

"My son and I will make the journey with you," Runs-Far said. "We will go with you to Shiloh to find my daughter, Chickadee, and her daughter, and all those linked to them. Our kindred."

Thomas raised a brow at Blue-Jay, who nodded as his father added, "They must know of us, these ones of ours. And they must be told of Sedi—Walnut—the mother of their clan."

Ayeli

At the Center

LONGMEADOWS PLANTATION

When Runs-Far's morning pipe drew to his satisfaction, he handed the glowing wood splinter to a sleepy-eyed Annie, who had lit it for him at the cookhouse hearth. While she yawned, he thanked her, then walked through the predawn half-light, down shadowed paths between fenced gardens, beyond to where the dewy grasses wet his moccasins. He walked until he reached the edge of a field planted in rolling lines of the plant he smoked, their leaves young and tender.

He stood in the morning's cool as the Green Corn Moon set new behind him, looking across the river—called James by the unega—to the wooded bank beyond where mist hung. Visible through it, the ghostly shapes of a dozen deer passed along, browsing as they went. The call of ducks, awake and squabbling on the water beyond, disturbed the stillness before the day broke.

Runs-Far listened, watched, and waited. For the sun to rise. For his son to come. As he had waited each morning since that son was old enough to take up a pipe and send his prayers to Creator with its smoke. Never yet had Blue-Jay joined him. While he waited, he prayed, unconcerned with being overheard.

"I give thanks, Creator-Father, for the path I have followed since it led from the place you raised me up to complete the journey left unfinished. I give thanks for clearing the path before me and for those you used to clear it—let blessing find each one in their need. I ask you to keep on clearing that path I see running on ahead of me yet a way."

He pulled on the pipe's stem, sent smoke to drift away, then raised the pipe toward the east, the direction of triumph, showing the dawn's first hint of red.

"S'gi." *Thank you.*

With his free hand he fished inside the bag he wore slung over a shoulder. He took out the turtle shell rattle, finished now. He had not chosen for its handle beech, a wood sacred to his own Longhair Clan. He had chosen maple, to honor the clan of his wife and children. Bird Clan.

He thought more on how the rattle was made, the hands that had contributed. Esther, who found the shell. Tamsen, who named those in the shops to ask for the things he needed to make the shell into what it had become. Those who gave sinew, rawhide, hemp rope, the maple, and the bits of rabbit fur. The children he had sent to the river to gather pebbles, Tamsen's daughters and one of Annie's. His own hands that put all the pieces together.

Hands from Turtle Island. Hands from Africa. Hands of white people. Each a different shade of Creator's image. *From every tribe and tongue...*

"S'gi." He shook the rattle to hear its sound. Pleased with it, he blessed it to its purpose and prayed for the day he could put it to its use. For now, he returned it to the bag. He drew on the pipe, breathed out its smoke, and started to sing.

It was a new song, one that had been stirring in his heart since they learned of Chickadee and her daughter, and that one's son. Of the one called Ian Cameron and those former slaves he had led north to freedom. Malcolm. Naomi. Ally. On this morning, the song chose to start taking its shape. He let it.

"Every tribe and tongue of us will sing your praise, Creator-Father,
With the blanket of Creator-Jesus's blood red around our shoulders.
Let all Peoples stand and praise you. Amen!

Black and Red and White, all Peoples bear your image, Creator-Father,
With the walls between us broken down by Creator-Jesus's blood.
Let all Peoples dance and—"

"Edo'da? What is this song you sing?"

Caught up in the song-birthing, Runs-Far had not heard the approaching footsteps long awaited. His son! His son had come to him, prayer pipe in hand, its stone bowl glowing like the sun now rising. Past the knot of joy and compassion in his throat he said, "It is a new song, giving itself voice. But it is for another day. Have you come to pray with me?"

Blue-Jay's amber eyes were raw. "If you will have me."

"Of course I will. Osda." *It is good.*

"S'gi."

His son was thanking him? "*Hawa.*" You are welcome. "Let us talk with Creator and share our hearts with Him and hear His."

With tears running down their faces, for the first time they stood together as men and welcomed the day, their backs to the place called Long Meadows, its people and animals astir now, making their morning sounds.

Somewhere a rooster crowed.

As Runs-Far peered sidelong at his son, who prayed in silence, eyes shut, his heart swelled with rejoicing. Much as he had put in his song, a wall that had long stood between them had crumbled in recent days. Still the lines across his son's brow scored deep while he prayed. Many wounds had this child of Runs-Far's heart suffered in his fifty winters. Many losses. Two wives. Two children. A mother. What was it hurting him now?

He would be missing the woman who had been his second wife, the one he had known longest, but a few moons gone. But Runs-Far suspected it was something more besides. He prayed until a warmth bloomed over the skin of his face, then opened his eyes. Across the river the sun was shooting golden arrows through the upper branches of the trees, down through the mist to pierce the tobacco rows, into which the fieldhands were making their way, calling to each other in snatches of their own songs. From an open window in the brick house behind them, an infant's cry drifted on the morning air. Its twin's voice joined it.

Runs-Far thought about his youngest child, this daughter he journeyed toward. Chickadee was no longer the baby he had carried in his mind. By turning back all those years ago, at MacKinnon's Cove, he had missed that baby. And the girl. And the young woman. But a woman in the fullness of her life yet lived, a new bride yet already one of the grandmothers—still somehow timeless to him—and he was going to her.

As was his Walnut's firstborn, standing beside him now in prayer, this one who had been as a son to him since he was himself barely a man. Blue-Jay had agreed to go with him to Shiloh, to find his sister and her offspring, though Runs-Far could see his heart was not whole concerning it.

Was it something more about Chickadee that was troubling him?

Though he could not think why that should be, Runs-Far offered up a final prayer before they went back among the people of that place. To Tamsen and Ambrose, Thomas and Esther. A prayer meant for Creator-Father's ears alone.

Make straight the path of my son. Make whole his heart. Heal the wounds over which he may yet stumble…

10

Tihaluhiyi — Green Corn Moon (June)

Another seven days passed before they were certain Thomas's fever would not return for the present. It was unusual, he told them, for such fevers to plague him more than once or twice in a year's span. This was the first it had caught him with an escaped slave in his charge.

"No doubt that is why our paths crossed," Blue-Jay heard his father tell Thomas the day before they were to resume their journey north. "You had need of us, and we of you. Now we will go on together. To Shiloh."

Not just the four of them, to begin with. Jesse Kincaid, with his wolf-dog, had returned to Long Meadows and with great surprise met his sons, born early but thriving. Jesse had meant to take his wife and children home to the mountains, but Tamsen said she was not ready to make that journey, and had he not left Cade and the boys to see to the planting? Ought Jesse to consider traveling at least a little distance with Blue-Jay and his wagon-full?

Blue-Jay could not deny he was relieved when Jesse agreed to accompany them along what had once been the Warrior's Path for many peoples—now the road through Virginia's Great

Valley—all the way to the border of the next state to the north, Maryland, and the river they would cross there, these days called Potomac.

"If you'll drive the wagon," Jesse suggested, "I'll let you do the talking as much as you will. It'll come easier with practice. Reckon we'll reach the Potomac in a fortnight, half that time again before you'll see me back," he added to Tamsen.

She assured him she would be ready by then to start for their mountain home—mountains Blue-Jay wondered whether he and his father would ever set foot upon again. This he kept to himself. Creator had seen them safe so far by means unforeseeable, but there was much ground to travel, more challenges to overcome.

To help with that, Ambrose Kincaid had his carpenter raise sturdy bows over the wagon's bed and cover them with canvas that would protect Runs-Far and Esther from sun and rain and slave-catchers' eyes. Ambrose also gave provisions to see them through the weeks remaining of their journey. Flour and cornmeal, sugar and beans, tea and salt, parched corn and bacon and dried fruit, along with things needed for cooking all that food. For it all, and for Thomas's care, Blue-Jay gave the gold John Reynold had sent to Ian Cameron.

It was with a very different heart that Blue-Jay stood with the others to bid Long Meadow's master farewell than had beat in his chest the morning he drove the wagon into that place, seeking his help.

Runs-Far put a hand to Ambrose's arm and spoke words of affirmation over the new path his life was soon to take.

Jesse's horse was saddled and waiting. Runs-Far and Esther climbed into the wagon's bed, now under canvas. The girl was dressed in her boys' clothes, easier for getting in and out of a wagon, though she was pleased with the petticoat and short-gown, stockings, shoes, and stays the woman, Annie, had fitted for her.

To Annie, the carpenter, and all those who lived out back of the big house they said good-bye, leaving them in a state of high spirits. They had heard they were not long destined to be slaves.

Thomas had been about to shake Ambrose's hand and climb onto the wagon's driving bench, where he would sit with Blue-Jay, when they caught the flash of a tawny body leaping through the air and heard a screech from inside the wagon.

"Dargo!" Jesse hurried to the canvas opening to haul his wolf-dog out of the wagon, into which it had leapt straight off the ground. "You all right in there?"

Blue-Jay joined Jesse, peering in to be sure his father was unharmed.

Runs-Far shook with silent laughter as Esther cowered from the big dog that turned a circle, smacking her in the face with its bushy tail.

"Why's that wolf in here?" she asked. As if in answer, the animal sat on its haunches beside her, put its hairy face next to her smooth one, and gave her cheek a sloppy lick. "Eee-ew!" She slapped a hand to her face. "Save me being 'et by a wolf!"

Apparently able to save herself in the situation, she put her hands to the dog's thick-ruffed shoulder and shoved, moving it over a hand's breadth.

"Not like it ain't already tight in here," she said, but hid a grin as the dog's tongue lolled again in a wide, self-satisfied smile.

"I'll take him out with me," Jesse said. "Or make him stay here with Tamsen." He started to lower the wagon's tail.

Esther stopped him. "He all right... I guess. Long as he don't take to licking me every time I turn around." She reached a tentative hand and patted the big dog's head.

With that settled, Ambrose spoke a final word to Thomas Ross. "Will I see you again?"

Thomas grinned, though his gaze was searching. "God and you willing. Before winter if I don't spend it in Shiloh with the rest of these folk. Thank you, for everything."

Ambrose nodded. "I expect you will find me, and this place, somewhat altered by the winter. Or should I say *thee* will find?"

Jesse tossed his head back with a laugh. "My cousin's turning Quaker. I did not see that coming. The Almighty has Himself a sense of humor, don't He?"

"Creator does." Blue-Jay shook the hand of Ambrose Kincaid, who had promised that upon Jesse's return he would introduce his cousin to the one for whom he was making such sweeping changes to his life, and the lives of those who served him. The woman he meant to marry.

Tamsen and her daughters appeared on the steps of the house. Blue-Jay waited with the wagon's traces in hand for Jesse to share a round of kisses before he mounted his horse and led the way down the main drive, past the sprawling fields of Long Meadows.

NORTHERN NECK OF VIRGINIA

There was plenty to be nervous about, but Blue-Jay was as prepared to meet what lay before him as he could be. He had silently encouraged himself as he stood with his father beside the Potomac River, where they smoked their pipes and prayed to Creator for the day to come—which would begin with loading the wagon onto the nearby ferry and crossing that river into Maryland.

Blue-Jay had not realized until their cookfire was doused, the team hitched, and the last belongings stowed, how much he had come to depend on Jesse Kincaid over the lengthening summer days they had traveled between the mountains through

Virginia—almost as much as Esther seemed to have become attached to the man's dog. The animal had held off strangers from the girl more than once when she had strayed too far from camp, or someone had approached it with no good intent, while the rest of their backs were turned.

Though chary of it at first, Esther was now rarely out of arm's reach of the dog, the two riding in the wagon bed, watching the dust of their passing settle into the grooved track behind them.

No one was quick to climb into the wagon to start their journey that morning, though the ferry was docked and waiting. Jesse stood with his horse saddled, the rest gathered close after the smoking and praying were done. He put a hand to Blue-Jay's shoulder, searched his face, and must have seen the misgivings Blue-Jay was trying to hide.

"You'll do fine. You ain't needed me for days, talking to those we've met and doing business along the way as if you were born among such folk. I've every confidence you'll see this lot safe to that farm you're aiming for."

A farm called Beech Spring, on Black Kettle Creek, near the village of Shiloh, in western New York. That was all they knew of the place Blue-Jay's niece, Seona, was now living.

"I'll be ready to hiss a word in your ear if you get stuck," Thomas said with that bold grin Blue-Jay could still find unsettling.

It was true his tongue still tripped over many English words. He could never make himself sound like a native speaker, but what Jesse had said before leaving Long Meadows had proved true. He had grown more proficient, forced to practice daily, for the road they traveled was full of others heading south and north, with towns and villages and creeks to ford along the way. There had been people who had needed help and Blue-Jay, Jesse, and Thomas had given it where they could. Taken it, when offered.

Runs-Far did not speak a word of reassurance, but the confidence in his eyes spoke more eloquently, and touched Blue-Jay more deeply, than did the words of the other two. He thought of Ambrose Kincaid, as he had often done since leaving Long Meadows, pondering how that man was changing his ways. Just as Blue-Jay had been forced to do, step by step, on this journey he had not wanted to make.

"Sometimes it is good for a man to walk in shoes that are strange to him," he admitted. "Even if they do not fit like one's own. That is a thing I am learning." He looked down at his feet, encased not in moccasins but a white man's stiff leather shoes, given him by Ambrose. The coat and breeches he wore, made of good brown cloth that made him appear a man of some means—as the unega counted such things—had been likewise given, but his ability to speak with confidence to white men he had learned from Jesse.

The man who operated the ferry boat, grown impatient, called out to know whether they meant to cross that morning or not.

Esther climbed into the wagon. Blue-Jay helped Runs-Far in behind her. Jesse mounted his horse and called for his dog. The dog did not appear.

"Where's he got to?" Jesse gazed along the riverbank as if expecting to see the big wolf-dog sniffing about somewhere.

Blue-Jay knew where that dog was. He nodded toward the back of the wagon's canvas.

Jesse dismounted to fetch his dog. Blue-Jay peered in too to see Dargo nestled under Esther's arm. The animal beat its tail when it saw Jesse at the wagon's rear. "Come on," he told the dog, but the animal did not obey his command.

"I ain't holding him back...just saying good-bye." Esther burst into tears and threw her other arm around the dog, who made a deep-chested sound like a groan.

"Hey now. Let's not set him to howling and spook the horses." Jesse studied the girl and the dog. Blue-Jay caught the understanding in his gaze, and the sorrow that flashed before he quirked a grin and said, "Dargo?"

At his name, the dog's ears swiveled toward Jesse.

"She your girl now?"

Dargo licked Esther's tear-stained face.

Jesse's voice thickened. "All right then. You stay."

Esther stopped crying and released the animal. "You mean it? He can come with me?"

"Aye, he can. He'll guard you well." Jesse swallowed then laid his hand on the dog's broad head. "Take care of each other."

Esther's arms snaked around the animal again. "We will. Thank you, Mister Jesse!"

So it was that, in the fullness of the Green Corn Moon, Blue-Jay brought his father, a wolf-dog, a runaway girl, and the man who had stolen her, across the Potomac River into Maryland. Safe on the northern bank, he pulled the wagon aside to make way for other traffic and for a last look back across the river. On its southern bank, Jesse Kincaid sat his horse, watching to be sure they made it over.

Beside Blue-Jay on the wagon bench, Thomas gave a shout that carried across the water.

Jesse raised his hat.

Blue-Jay raised a hand. Then he turned the team to follow the path leading away again, and the wagon rolled northward over the road to Shiloh.

11

Galoni — End of Fruit Moon
(August)

SHILOH, NEW YORK

With weather sticky-hot and often drenched by summer rain, the remainder of their journey took the rest of Green Corn Moon and all of Ripe Corn Moon. It was early in the End of Fruit Moon—called *August* by Thomas—when the tired wagon team turned onto the track that led away from a broad creek called West Canada, which they had traced many miles north from the Mohawk River, to follow another creek eastward into rising foothills. A woman washing garments in that creek said it was the one they sought, Black Kettle. The place called Shiloh, she assured them, would be found upstream.

It had been morning when they met that woman. The sun was past its highest point and starting down the sky, and all were sweating with the canvas sides of the wagon rolled high, when they lurched over the last rough bit of track and rattled into a village.

Blue-Jay's heart began to race. There was a blacksmith shop, identified by the *clink* of hammering. Up on a rise where the creek they had followed came falling was a mill, below which cabins and a few board houses were scattered over mostly level ground. Beyond these, forested ridges rose. Not terribly steep or high. Not mountains, as Blue-Jay had lived among all his life, but the beginnings of them.

Blue-Jay asked, "What do you think?"

Beside him on the driving bench, Thomas said, "Shiloh. Must be."

The relief sweeping through Blue-Jay had nothing to do with his certainty of the welcome this place had in store—he was still in doubt of that. Despite what John Reynold had said on the matter, it weighed on him that he had spent the gold meant for Ian Cameron. How would the man take such news? Would he consider Blue-Jay a thief? But he had done as he had promised in one matter: he had seen his father to this place. He hoped it would not prove a disappointment.

"We best get direction." Thomas climbed down from the wagon after Blue-Jay halted it near the smithy. "I've no notion where we'll find Ian's farm from this point."

Outside another structure several white men were gathered in the shade of an oak tree, some with cups or flasks in hand. That would be the tavern or trade store. Probably both. Such places were the heart of unega settlements. Sometimes also a meeting-house. Blue-Jay did not see one of those in this place.

Thomas was waiting for him to speak to the men gathered under the oak. More than one had regarded their arrival. Recalling that he was, in their eyes, head of this group of travelers, Blue-Jay started to climb down from the wagon, while Esther, his father, and the dog gazed at what could be seen of the village from the open-sided bed. Blue-Jay had one boot on the earth when a voice over at the oak rose louder than the few still talking.

"What on earth—Thomas Ross!"

"Mister Ian?" Esther scrambled from the wagon, Dargo leaping out after her.

Undaunted by sight of the long-legged creature on the girl's heels, the man who had called Thomas's name came striding toward them as Blue-Jay got both feet planted, wiped a sleeve across his sweating brow, and turned to face him.

Like Thomas Ross, the man had not yet seen thirty winters. His head was uncovered, his tailed hair sun-bleached to many shades of gold. He wore the sturdy plain shirt and breeches of a farmer, but no coat in the heat of the day. His well-made features revealed a disbelieving joy as he met Thomas with the unhesitating embrace of a brother.

"Ian," Thomas said as they parted. "Mighty fine to see you again."

"Aye, it is—though I can hardly credit it. And ... Esther!"

The girl was all but hopping up and down in her excitement, a feeling the dog had caught, causing her to grab its ruff so it did not leap up and dance as it was wont to do in greeting. "Mister Ian. I'm here!"

"So I see. I was going to ask how ye managed to find me, but I'm guessing John Reynold had a hand in that."

"He did! Miss Cecily too. And Mister Charlie and—" Esther broke off as the dog wriggled loose of her hold. "Dargo—sit!"

The dog half-obeyed, hovering beside Esther, ready to spring again. Ian Cameron eyed the dog, which eyed him back. "Can I give ye a hug, or will your wolf take it amiss?"

"Dargo's just part wolf. Let him get a sniff of you first."

The man stepped close to the dog, which Esther warned to mind his manners. The animal sniffed the sun-browned hand extended toward his muzzle, then brushed the dirt with his tail.

"Aye, a bonny great monster ye are," Ian Cameron crooned. "Welcome to Shiloh," he added, taking in Esther and Thomas as well. "Seona ... she'll be beside herself with happiness to see ye both, won't she?"

"I can't wait to see her!" Beaming and crying both, Esther threw her arms around Ian Cameron's waist, hugging him while he patted her back.

He was frowning when they parted. "Your parents, lass? Are they not with ye?"

Esther shook her head, sniffling and wiping tears. "Mama sickened and passed. Daddy got sold. Thomas got me away from Chesterfield. Miss Rosalyn... she caught us leaving, then you'll never guess—she let me go!"

The man's brows arched high. "Did she?"

"She did, and with a message for *you*," Thomas said, then looking around at his audience added, "It'll keep."

"Aye." Ian Cameron turned his attention to Blue-Jay, noticing Runs-Far in the wagon. "Who are these with ye?"

Blue-Jay had dreaded this moment, imagining it many ways. But the man with the unguarded smile Thomas led over to the wagon's bed did not match a single image he had entertained since learning of him.

"Ian. This is Runs-Far and his son, Blue-Jay, of the Cherokee people. Our companions on the journey."

Blue-Jay did not lower his gaze as Ian Cameron took in their faces, with the adjustment of thoughts flitting across his eyes Blue-Jay was used to seeing when he was made known as Tsalagi. The disparity between his appearance and identity did not seem to stumble the man. His gaze was open, his mouth still smiling.

"Good to meet ye both." He turned his focus on Runs-Far, who was peering out through the raised canvas. "Grandfather? D'ye speak English?"

Esther pushed in close. "He does. Good English."

"Ye've journeyed a long way from home, aye?" Ian Cameron asked Blue-Jay's father. "What brings ye so far north—and how did ye and your son come to be in company with these two?"

"That is a long story," Runs-Far said, "which I am sure one of us—or all of us—will be happy to tell."

"For now," Thomas said, "what you need to know about these two is that Runs-Far is Lily's daddy. Blue-Jay's her brother."

Ian Cameron's jaw fell slack. He blinked at Runs-Far. "Her father? How? I mean…"

That the man was caught off guard was clear enough. Blue-Jay watched his face, to know whether the surprise was a good one.

"They left their mountains early in spring," Thomas explained. "Found their way to Mountain Laurel—what's left of it. Charlie Spencer took them to John and Cecily. I was there at the time, liberating Esther, planning to head north to you in hopes of your aiding us. We've traveled together since."

Ian stared a moment longer, then reached into the wagon's bed to clasp the hand of Runs-Far. "I called ye Grandfather out of respect, but now I do so in truth. Lily's daughter, Seona—your granddaughter—is my wife."

"We know this," Blue-Jay said.

"Of course." Ian glanced at him, nodding. "That's why ye're here. And ye…Blue-Jay?" Shock was beginning to fade from the man's face, leaving room for what looked like pleasure seeping in to fill it. "Lily's brother?"

"We had the same mother," Blue-Jay said. "Lily is my sister."

Ian's grin blazed again. "That makes ye my uncle—at least how I reckon things." He held out his hand in the way of the unega. Hiding his misgivings, some of which were—he was himself stunned to realize—crumbling away, Blue-Jay took it in his own. A firm grasp, welcoming. Accepting?

"You have spoken of my granddaughter, Seona." Runs-Far leaned close to the wagon's bows. "What of Tsigalili? Is she also with you?"

"Aye," Ian Cameron said, and Blue-Jay caught the joy rising in his father's eyes, before the other man doused it. "I mean, no. She was." Again he shook his head. "Forgive me. I'm that astonished by your arrival—gladdened, to be sure. But Lily and Joseph—her husband—they left us last autumn for Grand River, meaning to stay the winter among Joseph's Mohawk kin. We've been expecting them all summer—for the wedding."

"Wedding?" Esther piped up. "Who's marrying?"

Ian spared her a grin. "My sister, Catriona."

"She came west with you?" Thomas asked. "Who's she marrying?"

"Our neighbor, Matthew MacGregor." Ian turned back to Blue-Jay and Runs-Far. "We expected Lily and Joseph to return in time but the wedding's tomorrow. I hope they still mean to come." Gaze shifting back to Thomas, he added, "My parents are here, all the way from Boston. They'll be glad to see ye again, Thomas."

"And Naomi?" Esther asked. "Ally? Malcolm? They here too, aren't they?"

Ian Cameron laughed. "They are. It's a right crowd we've assembled at the farm. I'm only in the village because Naomi ran out of sugar and still needs to bake the wedding cake."

Esther's eyes rounded, filling again with tears. "That white cake with the sugar-icing? Like she made for the big house at Mountain Laurel? She'd let me sneak a taste of that icing…"

"Ye can ask her yourself," Ian Cameron replied. "Let me fetch my horse, over at the smithy. If ye're ready to press on?"

"We're ready," Thomas said with a nod at Blue-Jay, who saw he was fast becoming no longer the man in charge of things. Glad to give that place to whomever wished to take it, he nodded, wanting to have this journey ended, his father united with his granddaughter. Though not with Chickadee.

Would his father be satisfied, or was this journey not yet over for them? And how was he to tell Ian Cameron that he had spent his gold?

While the man led over a sturdy roan gelding and Esther and the dog got back into the wagon, Blue-Jay peered at his father, still sitting in the wagon's depths, not looking back at him. Runs-Far's gaze seemed to have turned inward.

Whatever he was thinking, his face gave no indication.

Ian Cameron had spoken true. After Blue-Jay drew the wagon to a halt in the yard of the farm called Beech Spring, what could be considered *a right crowd* soon gathered.

This yard was shared by three cabins, a pole shelter covered in canvas, and, on a nearby rise, what would soon be a house larger than the cabins and shelter all joined together. It had a stone foundation and was framed up tall with two floor levels. Only the lower had walls put up. Milled lumber lay in piles around it, as well as more gathered stones. For the moment work had paused.

Spreading away from the cabins and the half-built house was a handsome stand of trees. Beeches mostly, some maples, here and there a birch. Beyond that lay fields of corn, the northern end of a lake they had just driven past, and then a long ridge, thickly timbered.

"Seona and I and the bairns are sleeping up at the house for the time being," Ian had said from the back of his horse as they came in sight of the farm. "My parents have our cabin. My sister, Catriona, will be leaving hers after the wedding tomorrow, going to live with Matthew, so that one will be empty. For tonight we'll find ye beds where we can, but ye're welcome to them."

By the time Blue-Jay had the wagon parked and Ian Cameron dismounted his horse, persons of varying ages had emerged from the cabins or the garden nearby. Blue-Jay hung back, helping his father from the wagon's bed after Esther and the dog tumbled out and raced across the yard to greet a brown-skinned giant of a man who had been mending garden pales.

"Ally! Ally, it's me!"

"Esther?" The big man had left off his work but halted in amazement while two rough-coated collies ran excited circles with the lanky wolf-dog. "That *you*? You done got bigger."

The girl's laughter rang, high and free, a sound Blue-Jay had rarely heard. "It's been a while, Ally. Those your collies?"

"Yep. I done trained 'em up to work the cows." Childlike pride shown from the big man's face. "They's named Nip and Tuck. What's this big fella you brung called?"

"Dargo. He's—" It was all Esther got out before a dark-skinned, heavy-set woman who resembled the man though older, appeared in one of the cabin doors, wiping her hands on a rag. A grease-spotted apron covered the faded calico front of her ample gown and skirt.

"What's going on out here?" she inquired before her gaze landed on Esther.

Dropping the rag, the woman clutched the cabin's doorframe. Then with a mighty shout she leapt into the yard, dancing herself to the girl, sturdy feet in worn shoes pounding the earth for joy—a display that made Runs-Far, on his feet in time to see it, laugh soft and deep in his throat. While the rest—Ian Cameron, two older white people who must have been his parents, the big man called Ally, Thomas, Blue-Jay, and Runs-Far—looked on, the girl was encompassed in the dancing woman's arms, never minding the heat of the day.

"Naomi," Esther moaned, laughter giving way to weeping in the woman's embrace. "I made it—I found you! But my mama's dead. Daddy got sold. I ain't got people no more. Just this big ol' *dog*," she added in a wail, as Dargo broke off greeting the collies and rushed to her side.

"Lord, help," the woman, Naomi, said, clutching at Esther. "That ain't no dog—that a *wolf*. He your wolf, baby girl?"

"Uh-huh." Esther wiped a hand beneath her tear-swollen nose. "He ain't a danger. Ain't never harmed chickens or nothing. He eats what I give him."

The dog sat and grinned, white teeth agleam.

With a wary eye on the animal, Naomi said, "Well... our chickens are put up, so never mind." Taking Esther by the shoulders, she looked the girl in the eye. "Listen to me now. I don't know what all's happened to you, child, but you wrong about having no people. I never forgot you. Never stopped praying. You be *my* girl now—if'n you want to be."

Blue-Jay heard his father's grunt of satisfaction, but his attention was caught by a figure standing in the doorway of a cabin behind his father—a woman with curling dark hair a little disheveled, as if she had just risen from a nap. By the way she was craning her head, the wagon and team blocked her view of the other cabin and those outside it.

She was young. Her tousled hair tumbled past her shoulders like a thundercloud. Her eyes were a startling green. Despite those eyes and skin that was not coppery like his father's—it was barely darker than Blue-Jay's—he could see glimpses of the Aniyunwiya echoed in the bones of her face. Glimpses of his own father's face.

A sleepy frown creased her brow. "Ian, who have you brought home? More wedding guests?"

Not until she stepped from the cabin did Blue-Jay realize the young woman was big with child. Very near her time. Two more children, a boy and girl—each about four summers in age—rushed out of the cabin into the yard as Runs-Far turned to see her there.

Then Esther rounded the wagon. "Seona!"

Astonishment swallowed the young woman's frown. "Esther?"

There was again much exclaiming, more laugher, more tears. Then the woman spotted Thomas. Her face, which Blue-Jay decided was one of the most beautiful he had ever seen, split again with joy.

He and his father waited as another reunion took place, then the older white man and woman, Robert and Margaret Cameron, were introduced to Esther. It was explained that Ian's sister, who was to be married, was at their neighbors, the MacGregors', farm.

Esther asked, "Where's Malcolm?"

"Inside," Ian told her, with a nod toward the cabin Naomi had come out of. "He's likely abed, but he'll have heard this hullabaloo."

"He will have," Naomi said, taking the girl in tow. "Come on. I'll take you to him."

That left everyone turning to look at Blue-Jay and Runs-Far. With the import of the news he was about to share clear in his expression, Ian put his arm around the shoulders of the green-eyed young woman and steered her over to them, his parents following. He nodded first at Blue-Jay and spoke his name, and that of his wife, whose name Blue-Jay did not need to be told.

"Welcome to Beech Spring," Seona Cameron said, smiling with her mouth, still questioning with her eyes, which had widened at his name. "What brings you here?"

"*You* bring me here," Blue-Jay told her. "You and your children. And your mother, though I am told Tsigalili is no longer here with you."

As his sister's daughter stared at him, it struck Blue-Jay that, aside from Redwing's grown children, she was the nearest to a daughter he would ever again know. In some ways closer than a daughter, for she was of his clan as his own children could never be. And she did not know it. She had no knowledge of her clan, her lineage, or of Sedi, the woman who had been her grandmother.

"How do you know my mama—much less the name *her* mama gave her?" Seona asked, blinking those green eyes in surprise.

"He knows of Lily," Ian said. "But they've never met. This is her brother, born before your grandmother, Sadie, was taken from their village and wound up at Mountain Laurel."

Seona's hand rose to cover her mouth. It hovered there a moment, then she removed it to say, "Mama's *brother*? My Grandma Sadie was your mother too?"

Blue-Jay started to speak, but at this point, Runs-Far could no longer keep quiet. "Not Sadie. *Sedi.* Walnut, you would say. That is the name I gave her soon after we found her, the day this one was being born," he added with a nod at Blue-Jay, who watched his sister's daughter turn her attention to his father.

He tried to see Runs-Far through her eyes, as if for the first time. His father was not a tall man—neither of them were as tall as Ian Cameron—but Runs-Far was still straight and carried no spare flesh, even at his belly. He wore his leggings and breechclout, but that morning he had donned his best linen shirt with the ruffles down its front, and the silver arm bands he saved for the best occasions. He had also tied the feathers of a heron into his long gray hair. He had donned his good moccasins, the ones with quilled designs, and a necklace Blue-Jay had not seen him wear in a very long time, from which hung a copper disk the size of a man's palm, engraved with the symbol of a fish that those who followed Creator-Jesus had known from ancient times, in far-off places. His warm brown face with its wide brow and prominent cheekbones was deeply lined from nose to mouth, and at the corners of the dark eyes set into his face exactly like those of the granddaughter he now faced, with a slight up-tilt at their outer corners. His father's eyes were bright, shimmering in the sunlight of the cabin yard, where all the people stared.

"And you are?" Seona asked, but Blue-Jay was certain she had guessed, for she gripped the arm of her husband hard, her other hand resting across her swollen belly.

"This is Lily's father," Ian said. "Your grandfather. He's called Runs-Far."

Runs-Far had been absorbing this first sight of Seona Cameron with the same intensity as she had been looking at him.

"Granddaughter," he said. "We have come a great distance from the mountains of our people to give you greeting. I bring the greetings of your aunt, Redwing, and of her children, and their children, which are growing to be many. I bring you greetings from all the aunts, uncles, brothers, and sisters of your clan."

"My … clan?" Seona echoed in a near-whisper.

"You are a daughter of *Anitsisqua*, the Bird Clan, one of the seven clans of The People," Runs-Far said. "As is Chickadee, your mother."

"And you've come with Thomas and Esther? Where …? How did …?"

Runs-Far smiled at Seona's half-formed questions. "I will tell you all you wish to know, how I and your uncle have come here. About your clan. About all the Tsalagi, a people you may claim as your own. You and Chickadee, who I have also come hoping to see."

"Mama …" Seona turned her wondering gaze up to her husband's. "Oh, Ian. Do you think they're still coming? Mama and Joseph?" Before he could give answer, she turned back to Blue-Jay and his father. "But you'll stay with us? Of course you'll stay! How *long* can you stay?"

Runs-Far drew breath to give a reply Blue-Jay very much wanted to hear for himself, but Esther appeared in the other cabin door, beckoning to Blue-Jay and his father.

"I done told Malcolm about you two. He's right keen to see you. Come inside!"

12

BEECH SPRING

With preparations for the wedding of Ian's sister busying everyone, there had been little chance for Blue-Jay and Runs-Far to speak long with those who called this place home, save to the two whose condition required they remain at rest.

One of those was Malcolm, who had spent most of his eighty years a slave at Mountain Laurel. The morning of the wedding, a bed was made under the pole-arbor so the old man could watch the doings of Naomi, Esther, and Willa MacGregor—mother of the man Ian's sister was marrying—and others from Shiloh making ready for the wedding feast. Tables were set in the yard between the cabins, in one of which Ian's sister was readying herself with help from her mother and Maggie MacGregor, sister of her soon-to-be husband. Chairs, benches, and makeshift stumps had been arranged at the edge of the beeches, where the ceremony would take place.

From his blanket beside Malcolm's pallet, Runs-Far observed the cabin yard and said, "There will be room enough, I think."

"Room for what, Edo'da?" Blue-Jay, seated cross-legged next to him, asked.

It was good to be under the arbor, out of the way but able to observe the people, most of whom were strangers still, though Ian Cameron had introduced Blue-Jay and Runs-Far to each.

MacGregors. Warings. Kepplers. MacNabs. More names of neighbors Blue-Jay could not remember.

"For the dancing," Runs-Far replied.

"Do these people dance at weddings?"

Malcolm had also been watching the yard where men stood talking, children played, and women moved between cabins. "Oh, aye," the old man said, his manner of speaking—as if he had been born in Scotland like the elder Camerons—still odd to Blue-Jay's ears. "They dance."

Though he did not think Malcolm could mean the type of dancing his father meant, Blue-Jay did not comment on it. In the short time they had known the man, they had learned much from him about Chickadee, for Malcolm had been the nearest thing to a father she had had. Blue-Jay's father had shared stories of Walnut, who Malcolm remembered—not just from that time she bore a baby and died of it. He remembered Blue-Jay's mother as the girl, Jemma, who had come with the Scotsman, Alex MacKinnon, when both fled that place on the Cape Fear River where he was indentured, she a slave.

"Even then she was set on finding her people. When she came again to us at Mountain Laurel, years later, 'twas plain she'd done it. Aye," Malcolm added, seeing their surprise. "I kent who she was. In a moment alone wi' her, as the bairn was coming, she bid me not to reveal her identity lest she be enslaved ag'in. She meant to take up her bairn and run, return to ye, soon as she'd the strength to do it. I meant to help her, but she died afore she got more than a glimpse o' her wee daughter. Not afore she spoke a name—or what we thought a name. Now we ken 'twas your word for *Chickadee*."

Until their arrival the previous day, Malcolm had kept his small knowledge of Chickadee's mother silent. There had been nothing in it to aid in discovering more about her and Seona's kin, no need to confirm that she was what they had always surmised, a runaway slave taken in and adopted by the Cherokee.

"How did you come to know the meaning of my daughter's name?" Runs-Far had asked, unashamed of the tears he shed, having found the one man in all the world who could tell them of Walnut's passing, of her heart at that moment. A heart undaunted. "How, if you never spoke of her to anyone?"

"We all kent what she called Lily—*Lily* being what we shortened it to. But we never kent its meaning until Lily joined us here and met the man she married, Joseph Tames-His-Horse Roussard. He's a Mohawk man but kent a bit of your tongue too. Enough to tell Lily the meaning of what her mama spoke with her last breath."

They had heard again the story of Ian and Seona, who appeared happy with her choice of husbands despite their shared, painful past. Still, Blue-Jay had not let down his guard concerning that man. He had yet to tell of the gold he had used, or the letter John Reynold had pressed upon him at their parting. Ian was preoccupied with hosting the wedding, and though Runs-Far went among these people with the ease of one born among them, Blue-Jay was keeping his distance. Taking their measure.

"Tell me again," Runs-Far said as Seona stepped from a cabin and made her way to where the wedding would take place, under the beeches. "How long is it since my granddaughter came to this place?"

As if she knew herself the topic of conversation, Seona glanced their way. Instead of taking a seat on one of the chairs set out, she approached them with her shifting gait, belly thrusting ahead like a basket full of corn held tight.

"Just o'er a year," Malcolm said. "Married to Ian since the autumn. I'm blessed to see them raising the bairns together. And another soon to join us," he added as Seona came within hearing of his throaty voice.

Chickadee's daughter was the other one Runs-Far and Blue-Jay had had time to talk with, for she had been forbidden by the other women to work because her time was so near. She had told them of her father, who died before she was born, that he had loved her mother, that he had been a man unlike his father, their former master—and Seona's grandfather. "Aidan Cameron didn't want to own slaves, Mama tells. Had he not died so young... things would've been different for us. Another thing Mama tells of my daddy, he was the sort to tame and tend wild creatures."

One of those had been a raven, raised from a chick, taught to eat from Aidan Cameron's hand. And taught the speech of men so it seemed it could carry on a conversation.

"In truth?" Blue-Jay could not stop himself asking. "The raven spoke?"

"True as Scripture," Seona said. "I knew that old bird, heard him for myself. Munin, he was called. Now and then he'd find me or mama in the forest, visit for a spell. You don't believe me, Grandfather?" she asked, catching Blue-Jay's father staring at her with his eyes wide and wondering.

"I do not doubt it," Runs-Far said. "Among the clans it is said the birds are ones who bring messages between the People and Creator. To the Bird Clan, then, falls the charge of caring for birds."

Seona smiled over that bit of knowledge of the people from who she came, in part. "But my daddy was Scottish, not Cherokee. He's the one who charmed the wild things. Not just birds. Deer, too."

Runs-Far had smiled, accepting the mystery of Aidan Cameron without the need to dig up its roots for understanding. "He would have been valued among the Aniyunwiya, your father."

Seona had much to tell them of her mother as well, stories of the many people Chickadee had healed with her knowledge of herbs and medicine, and the babies she had helped bring into the world as a slave in North Carolina, and as a free woman in New York—such as the little daughter of Willa MacGregor, toddling around on unsteady legs as the wedding preparations continued.

But the feats of Seona's mother were not limited to midwifery and medicinal teas. There was Neil MacGregor, adopted father of the young man who was marrying Ian's sister, standing there among the men talking. That man, himself a physician, walked with the aid of a cane, but he had a foot to walk on because of Lily's skill in repairing grave damage done it by the jaws of a hidden trap the man had stepped into, the previous year. And there was Ian himself, who Lily had saved back at Mountain Laurel when he had gone searching for Seona, thinking she had run away from him, and been attacked by that panther.

Seona had reached the pole-arbor. Runs-Far made to stand, maybe to give her his place, but she shook her head. "If I got down on that blanket, big as I am, I'd never get up again. Just have this baby right there."

She arched her spine as she spoke, rubbing at her lower back. Blue-Jay, his gaze at the level of her belly, felt his eyes pop wide.

Seona laughed. "Uncle, don't look alarmed. I promise this baby won't be coming today. I think so, anyway."

The address of *Uncle* filled Blue-Jay with pleasure. He liked this young woman with her smooth, not-quite-white skin, eyes like the mossy waters of a creek. He would have liked her even had she not been a clanswoman of his mother's blood.

"I'm just glad I'll be here to see it," Malcolm said. "I think so, anyway," he added with a tired smile, echoing Seona's words.

"You hang on now." Though her voice was light, Seona's smile dimmed with the sadness of a parting soon to come. "A little while longer."

"I am glad also to be here to see this new child born to Walnut's clan," said Runs-Far. "And for many other reasons, I am glad. This is a good day."

"It is, Grandfather." Seona reached down and took the hand of Runs-Far, raised to hers. "I just wish Mama would hurry up and get here. She'll be so…I don't know what all. Surprised—happy—there really are no words."

"Chickadee will be no happier than *I* will be," Runs-Far said.

"Amen," Malcolm said. "Reckon I could about get up and dance, myself, once the fiddlin' commences."

Seona laughed. Runs-Far smiled, anticipation in his eyes.

Blue-Jay wrestled down thought of his father's disappointment if Chickadee did not arrive—and dread over what he might wish to do about it. Not even the neighbors, the MacGregors, could explain why Chickadee and her husband had not yet come. Blue-Jay had been surprised to learn that not only was Ian's sister, Catriona, marrying a man who was half *Kanien'kahá:ka*, called Mohawks by the whites, but that that man's adopted white mother, Willa MacGregor, had been adopted herself by that people as a young person, made a daughter of the Wolf Clan. It was Willa's clan brother that Chickadee had married last autumn. Blue-Jay did not know if it was the same with the Kanien'kahá:ka but among the Tsalagi, Wolf Clan men were brave warriors, protectors of the People. It was a strong pairing his sister had made.

Conversations in the yard began to quiet, signaling the wedding was to begin. Runs-Far declared he would watch from the arbor which was near enough for Malcolm to see. Blue-Jay walked with Seona to the chairs under the beeches but chose to stand near the back with her.

"I cannot bear to sit so long," she had said, "and don't want to disrupt things with my moving around."

The ceremony soon began, led by an older man whose name Blue-Jay thought was Waring. *Colonel Waring.* Catriona Cameron, a woman younger than his niece, with russet hair like her father's and pale skin a contrast to her chosen husband with his brown skin and black hair tied back, stood before Colonel Waring and spoke their words of promise. A ring was put on Catriona's finger. A prayer was prayed. More words said. Then the young couple, she in a fresh new gown the shade of butter and he in his dark coat with tails, kissed one another in front of all those watching.

Blue-Jay's face warmed at the display. There was clapping, hooted calls from the youngest men. Margaret Cameron, the mother of Catriona and Ian, cried through her smiles. That seemed to be the end of it, except for the feasting. And the dancing Malcolm had promised, led by a man with a fiddle who stood on a stump after most had eaten their fill of the food prepared, much of it strange to Blue-Jay.

Though each person had taken a plate and sat wherever they wished to eat, again Blue-Jay had sheltered beneath the arbor with Malcolm, who sat up to eat a little and was visited by many.

Some spoke to Blue-Jay. Their connection to Seona and her children, and the absent Chickadee—Lily, to these people—was becoming widely known. But Blue-Jay did not enter conversations as readily as Runs-Far. He could not stop wondering what his father meant to do if Chickadee did not return to that place. He had tried to talk about it under the arbor the night before.

His father had wanted to talk about trees.

"Have you noticed the trees of this place?" he had asked as they stared into a sky strewn with stars.

"I have. What of them, Edo'da?"

"There are many beeches," his father said, naming the tree linked to his Longhair clan. "But that one big tree the husband of my granddaughter chose to build his house beside—that is a maple. The tree of my wife's clan. And they did not even know..."

His father's breathing had soon signaled sleep, but Blue-Jay had lain awake thinking of their journey and those met along its path. Most had helped them on their way: Cade and Jeremiah Ring; Joanna MacKinnon and Edmund; Charlie Spencer and the Reynolds; Tamsen, Jesse, and Ambrose Kincaid.

Others had tried to thwart them or helped for their own spiteful ends: Rosalyn and Gideon Pryce.

His thoughts recalled John Reynold's words about Ian Cameron. *Show Ian the grace you would desire, should anyone hold a wrong against you.* Those words had proved foretelling. It was he who might need to beg grace from Ian, not the other way around.

Now he looked for the man. Ian Cameron was not dancing to the fiddle's tune but standing outside the cabins with Thomas Ross. Recalling the letter John Reynold had given him—and the gold—Blue-Jay decided it was time to hand over the one and confess what he had done with the other.

Leaving his father with Malcolm and Seona's children, who had latched onto their great-grandfather, asking the endless questions that small children do, Blue-Jay rose and went to the wagon left parked outside the stable. He found the sealed letter in his bag, then turned back to the cabin yard, where the light was turning gold as the sun dipped westward.

Despite the warmth of the day, someone was building a fire near those dancing, a thing Blue-Jay now supposed would go on after darkness fell. Neither Ian nor Thomas heard his approach over the noise of fiddling and dancing or noticed him coming along the shadowed side of the cabin not facing the yard full of people.

When he came within sound of their voices he paused. Thomas was talking of bringing more slaves north.

"From now on I'll be taking them through to Canada. Would you be against my making Beech Spring a stopping place on that road?"

"Of course not," Ian replied. "Ye'll find help here, Thomas—and friendship—always."

It seemed a good point to interrupt, but Thomas spoke again. "Before I forget, I need to tell you what Rosalyn Pryce said, the night we liberated Esther. That message I'm meant to convey."

"It cannot be pleasant, but let's have it."

"*Tell him I have not forgiven him for breaking my sister's heart. I never will.* Those were her words. She also said to tell you that you were right. Know what she meant by that?"

"Aye, I think I do—her decision to marry Pryce. I warned her against the man, but it's no discussion for today." Ian watched those celebrating his sister's marriage, his mouth twisting in a smile. "The Almighty be thanked *His* mercies are new every morning, and that the sister Rosalyn holds such bitterness against me for wounding—knowing how I struggled letting Seona go—had a grasp on grace the likes of which I'll never meet again on this earth. Judith Bell Cameron died unfettered by resentment or blame, knowing as well how I'd grown to appreciate her. And love her. So now I choose *her* way. Grace undeserved, toward myself, as well as any who may cause me grief. I pray one day Rosalyn chooses likewise."

Taking in the words, Blue-Jay understood at last what sort of man his sister's daughter had chosen to marry. A man who had wrestled with his own failures and guilt and, in the end, fallen on the mercy of Creator-Jesus.

Whether it was his imagination, or a veil had lifted, Blue-Jay saw Ian Cameron standing before him with a righteousness not his own robing him in red, like a blanket-coat dipped in blood—an image from that song he had sometimes heard his father singing to himself since that first morning they had prayed together at Long Meadows. Ian Cameron was a man no different than Blue-Jay, one who had not always done right, even when he meant to do so. But his heart was made new, made good, and he was trying to live from that good heart—to hear Creator's voice and follow where He led.

"Blue-Jay?"

Startled from his thoughts by Thomas's address, Blue-Jay came forward, holding out the letter to Ian, who took it with a curious frown.

"This was given to me, for you. There was gold given as well, also meant for you, but with John Reynold's permission I used that gold for other needs on our journey to this place. I will repay. If that is what you wish."

Ian shook his head. "Thomas told me about the gold. I'm glad of the use to which ye put it—for Esther's sake, and this fellow's," he added with a good-natured shove at Thomas's shoulder. "In fact, he and I were just discussing—"

Outcries from the wedding guests arose, distracting Ian from what he had meant to say. At first Blue-Jay assumed it part of the dancing, or the music, until the fiddling stopped. The outcries continued.

"Look who's here at last." Ian turned Blue-Jay toward the narrow track that led between the corn standing at the field's edge, tall and ripening for harvest. No one had seen the approach of mounted riders until they had reached the head of the track, at the edge of the yard.

The first rider was a man sitting tall on a dun mare. He was lithe and well-muscled as a warrior though his hair, black as his horse's mane, was unshaven, falling long over his shoulders. The other was a slender woman on a darker horse, her skin lighter than the man's though still a coppery hue. From behind her the top of a cradleboard peeked. Already the warrior was off his horse and reaching long arms for that cradleboard, which he held while the woman dismounted.

It took but a glance for Blue-Jay to know who he beheld. Chickadee had come with her husband. And a baby.

Beside him, Ian Cameron loosed a shout. "Uncle Callum!"

He all but raced across the yard, Thomas behind him, for there was a third rider in the party, come out of the corn behind the other two leading his mount—a yellow-haired man already being embraced by Ian's mother, Margaret, who looked so like this new arrival it was plain even from that distance they were brother and sister.

Many voices exclaimed over the warrior, the woman and her child, the unexpected kinsman of the Camerons. Smiles of greeting wreathed many faces, but Blue-Jay wanted only to find his father, to stand beside him in this moment that would in truth end the journey begun far away in the mountains they called home.

Others were before him, taking that place.

Runs-Far stepped from the arbor, the children, Gabriel and Mandy, tugging him toward the woman who had taken her tiny baby out of its cradleboard and stood now with it in her arms as she was embraced by her grown daughter, near to giving birth herself, then Naomi, Esther, Catriona, Willa MacGregor, and others, until finally a path cleared, and all took note of the elderly man approaching.

Seona's children led their great-grandfather to meet his daughter, who Blue-Jay could see was being told by Seona who he was to them. Then Runs-Far was standing for the first time before Tsigalili of the Bird Clan, now called Lily Roussard.

The scene blurred as Blue-Jay's eyes filled with tears, yet he stood apart, like a tree rooted, and could not make his feet cross the ground to join them.

He joined them, of course, after his father had embraced his long-sought-for daughter and could bring himself to take his gaze from her and look for his son. Blue-Jay had met his sister, her kin and friends gathered around, happy for her wonder and surprise in arriving to find them there. He and his father had admired her baby, another daughter of Walnut's blood—reason for the late arrival. He had met Joseph Tames-His-Horse Roussard, the Mohawk warrior his sister had married. But he could not say now what words he had exchanged with either. Good words, they must have been, for his sister's smile had not faltered. Though tears had fallen as her gaze drank in his and their father's faces, Blue-Jay thought them tears of joy. They did not reach his heart, which he knew now had long been shut away inside a hardened shell, like that turtle's shell his father made into a rattle.

Chickadee settled amongst the wedding guests, baby in her arms. Food was offered her, while Joseph and the other man, Callum Lindsay, tended their horses. Ian, delighted by this uncle's arrival, helped with that. By the time they returned, and Joseph and Callum had eaten, the sun was setting.

Runs-Far, who had not left Chickadee's side since their meeting, now rose, leaving no barrier between Blue-Jay and his sister. Their father crossed the yard to where Ian stood talking with his parents and uncle. At a touch on his arm he stepped aside and gave Runs-Far his attention.

"Brother," said the sister sitting near. "Would you like to hold your niece?"

The baby, yet unnamed, had been a surprise to all. This daughter and Chickadee's grandchildren would grow up together, for Blue-Jay had heard someone saying Joseph Roussard had brought his little family back to this place to stay. But he did not want to hold the baby with her dark cap of hair and dusky skin that would be like her mother's. He did not want to be left alone with this sister whose face very much resembled Redwing's, who this one did not yet know about.

"I am not truly the son of that one," he blurted, nodding toward Runs-Far, talking with Ian, gesturing toward the fire, to which wood was being added, making the sparks fly upward.

Why had he said such a thing? He was more the son of Runs-Far than he had ever been the son of that white man who had caused him to exist. Runs-Far had had more to do with raising him than most men did their children, who belonged to their mother's clan and usually had their mother's brothers to teach and nurture them.

Walnut had had no brothers. Not even sisters. While some Bird Clan women—all mothers in the way of the Aniyunwiya—had stepped up to help, it had been primarily their father who cared for him and Redwing after their mother was taken, teaching Blue-Jay to hunt and fish, how to be a man.

"Were ye adopted?" Chickadee asked, surprising Blue-Jay.

"I was. When Runs-Far married our mother." He dropped his gaze to the sleeping baby in his sister's arms. "I was no bigger than that one. But I am what I look. Mostly white."

Chickadee blinked at the feathers he had tied in his graying hair, at the quilled vest and moccasins he had donned for this occasion. The trade-silver brooches adorning his clothing. She did not quite meet his gaze, as if she sensed his discomfort. "Like my girl-baby—my first one," she clarified, nodding to where Seona sat with the young women gathered around the new bride, Catriona. "Her daddy was white, with those pretty green eyes. She takes after him. But our mother? Ye remember her?"

"I do." Blue-Jay withheld his gaze from the sister who had lived when their mother died. That shell around his heart was growing smaller, tighter.

"Could ye tell me something of her?"

Blue-Jay was saved from answering when Ian Cameron gave a piercing whistle and, as conversations quieted, commanded everyone's attention.

"Grandfather Runs-Far asks a favor. He'd like to show us a dance of the Cherokees. A friendship dance, in honor of my sister's marriage, of Lily and Joseph's arrival, and the newest addition to our clan," he added with a grin shot in Blue-Jay's direction.

The grin was meant for Chickadee and her daughter, but Blue-Jay felt like a deer facing a hail of arrows as many gazes shot their way. Then he noticed what his father was doing. Runs-Far had moved to the fire and was talking to those nearest it. They began to clear a space around the flames. Esther came running and handed him the shell rattle he had made on the journey.

He'd like to show us a dance... Alarm shot through Blue-Jay as Ian's words sank in. Too late. Runs-Far already stood by the fire with his rattle, beckoning Blue-Jay forward. "Come, my son. Lead the dance with me. I will set the rhythm and sing, but your voice is stronger. Call them to the fire. To us."

Blue-Jay did not remember lurching to his feet or crossing the open space around the fire. He was suddenly at his father's side, heart thudding like a drum. "No one in this place knows our dances, Edo'da. Who will come at my call?"

With a look that saw deeper into his soul than Blue-Jay wanted him to see, Runs-Far put a hand to his arm. "Just begin it. Let Creator worry about what follows."

As his father gave the rattle its first shake, a familiar sound so out of place in that setting, Blue-Jay took in the faces encircling them, watching. Most were white, but not all. Some were the familiar red-brown of his own people, others darker.

The sun had set. Beyond the faces, twilight gathered. Blue-Jay saw the cabins and the unfinished house, the beeches that must have given the place its name, the tips of their boughs catching firelight, summer-green shimmered in gold. He felt the heat of the fire, the cooling of the day. A sheen of sweat bloomed over his skin.

Then he was doing as his father had bid, calling to those gathered in the ancient words of the Aniyunwiya, bidding them come and dance, to not leave him and his father standing alone.

At first that was what they did—left them standing alone. To Blue-Jay it felt an eternity while he called to these people who stared back at him blankly, or frowning, or grinning in amusement. None understood what he wanted of them, he thought.

Then Joseph Tames-His-Horse leaned close to Chickadee and spoke something that made her eyes widen. She rose, handed her sleeping daughter to a woman sitting near, and walked straight to the fire, to him, as Runs-Far lifted his voice in a song Blue-Jay knew for the one he had been composing since that morning at Long Meadows. The words were in Tsalagi.

> "Every tribe and tongue of us will sing your praise, Creator-Father,
> With the blanket-coat of Creator-Jesus's blood red around our shoulders.
> Let all Peoples stand and praise you. Amen!"

"I'll help ye get things started," Chickadee said when she reached him. "But I don't know the steps. Can ye show me?"

Blue-Jay looked down into eyes the same brown as their father's, dark and warm. His heart beat harder as he reached for her hand. With the other he took his father's hand, as Runs-Far shook the rattle and went on singing.

"It is simple. Follow us. Stomp your feet to the rattle's beat."

With Runs-Far leading, singing his song, they moved in a slow circle around the flames, their feet pounding the earth to the rattle's rhythm.

> "Black and Red and White, all Peoples bear your image, Creator-Father,
> With the walls between us broken down by Creator-Jesus's blood.
> Let all Peoples dance and praise you. Amen!"

Some of the faces watching now reflected uncertainty. Even unease.

Until Joseph Tames-His-Horse stood to his impressive height and told the people, "He is singing a song of friendship to celebrate this gathering—I understand some of it. It is also a song to the Almighty, a song of praise and thanks. He sings of every tribe and people praising Creator because of the blood of Jesus. It is a good song. I am going to join the dance. All are welcome!"

Before Joseph had stopped speaking his clan sister, Willa MacGregor, had risen, leaving her small daughter in the care of her husband. Joseph clasped the hand of Chickadee, Willa taking his other, both stomping in time to Runs-Far's rattle with the skill of those who had danced thus around many fires, as Blue-Jay's father sang on.

> "By great love and mercy you have called us from afar, Creator-Father,
> To gather as your clan, stained red beneath the cross of Creator-Jesus.
> Let all Peoples shout and praise you. Amen!"

Willa's newly married Mohawk son, Matthew, and his sister, Maggie, shared a grin then leapt from their places to join in. Not to be left out, Ian's sister followed, taking her new husband's reaching hand.

Ian joined the circle next. Callum Lindsay stood and bent a hand to Ian's mother. She shook her head, but Ian's father gave her a prod and, laughing, she let her brother pull her to her feet. They joined the dance.

Runs-Far led them in a faster circle. As Blue-Jay came around again, he saw Naomi and Esther helping Malcolm to his feet so he could shuffle toward the fire. The dancers parted, letting the old man come into their moving center, close to the flames. Esther and Naomi joined the stomping circle.

Still singing and shaking his rattle, Runs-Far broke away to stand with Malcolm, leaving Blue-Jay to lead the dancers.

> "We come as a bride to the marriage feast, called by Creator-Father,
> With our hearts made ready by Creator-Jesus's love.
> Let all Peoples drink, and eat, and praise you. Amen!"

More were joining the dance. Seona's children. Others Blue-Jay did not know. He led them around the fire, keeping it simple, not making their circle coil back upon itself as his people who knew this sort of dance would have done.

Hearing laughter near him, he looked down.

Chickadee's face glowed in the firelight. Her hand clung to his, their sweat mingling. She lifted her face to him. "Am I doing it right?"

"You are dancing well... Sister," Blue-Jay said. And with that word on his lips, he understood it was not the shell around his heart growing smaller but the heart within it growing larger. The sight of his sister dancing with joy swelled his heart enough to crack that shell wide, making room for her, as her heart had made room this day for him. For their father. For a People she did not yet know.

But she would know. He would tell her of them. He would tell her of their mother. Of her sister, Redwing, and that one's children and grandchildren. He would tell her what it meant to be Bird Clan. He would tell her everything she wanted to know. Probably more besides.

For now there was this dance, in which all were telling their story with pounding feet and gripping hands and faces aglow in the firelight they circled, while two old men stood in their center, one shaking his rattle and singing to Creator, the other holding fast to his arm, watching the familiar faces swirling past, moving on and on around the circle—much the way time flowed.

Theirs was the story of a kindred drawn from many nations, tribes, and tongues, as his father's song talked about. A taste of what was coming for all who followed Creator-Jesus down the narrow trail he blazed, from an atoning death to an empty tomb to a Kingdom where all would be made right and whole, toward which each of them journeyed. Each who clung to that atonement as tight as the hands around that circle.

For now the dance was enough. The hand and laughter and flashing dark eyes of a lost sister found was enough—more than enough—to fill the heart of a man that had long been broken but was beginning, at last, to mend.

Epilogue

BEECH SPRING

The names of Chickadee's daughter and Seona's son, born the morning after the wedding, were first spoken ten days after all had danced to Runs-Far's song.

They did this inside Naomi's cabin. Malcolm wished to be present but had not often left his bed since the wedding day. Most guests were long departed. Ian Cameron's sister had gone to where her new husband lived and worked, on a different farm on the other side of the village, Shiloh.

Even so, the cabin was full.

There was Malcolm in his narrow bed. Beside it stood Chickadee and Seona, their new ones cradled in their arms. Behind them stood Joseph Tames-His-Horse and Ian Cameron, his older children pressed close so as not to miss a thing.

On the other side of the bed stood Naomi, Ian's parents, and his uncle, Callum Lindsay. Those last three would be leaving on the morrow, the parents traveling to see another son and new grandchild, then back to their home in Boston. Callum would go in the opposite direction, back to his family in Canada.

Esther and the big child-man, Ally, stood at the bed's foot, Thomas and Blue-Jay with them. That left Runs-Far to stand nearest to Malcolm, who had been a father to Chickadee all the years he had not been part of his daughter's life.

Taking in their faces wreathed with smiles for these new ones, Runs-Far understood that his journey had been about more than the concerns of his own heart that began it. Those concerns were put to rest. He had learned of Walnut's fate. He had found their daughter. And so much more.

"Reckon this one's gonna have *your* hair, Seona." Esther craned to see the dark-capped head of the infant boy held in the arms of his mother, who smiled and bent a kiss to the baby's scrunched brow. "Maybe your eyes, too."

The journey had been about many paths coming together. Esther's was one. As was Thomas's.

The journey had been about the healing of many hearts, including the heart of his son, who was gazing at the sister Runs-Far suspected he had once feared finding with a shy pride and affection softening his face.

They were coming to know this lost one of theirs for themselves now, not just through the stories of others. She was a healer, a wise grandmother, a diligent worker. Strong of heart, like her mother before her. A true daughter of Walnut, who had run from slavery and found her people—found Runs-Far and chose to make a life with him, was giving to him still. This daughter and all her kindred.

Do you see this, my little wife? Do you see these daughters and sons of your blood? Listen! Bend your ear from Heaven. The names of these new ones are about to be spoken.

Malcolm was too weak to hold the babies so Runs-Far held them each in turn and lowered them for the older man to speak his blessing. Then their mothers spoke their names, loud for all to hear.

"Jemma Sedi Roussard," Chickadee said. "Daughter of the Bird Clan of the Aniyunwiya. Named for her grandmother."

"Aidan Malcolm Cameron," Seona said over her new offspring. "A son of the Cherokee Bird Clan."

Malcolm grinned at the namesake he shared with Seona's long-dead father. "Now I ken why the Almighty lengthened my days. So I might see this moment, in this place." His tired gaze moved across each face as he spoke, lifting last to Runs-Far, who heard between those words: *now I can depart in peace.*

Already Malcom was drifting back to sleep. He roused long enough for Blue-Jay and Thomas so say their farewells. Then, leaving him at rest, all went out into the summer warmth for more partings.

The wagon that had carried Runs-Far and Blue-Jay over many roads, across rivers, through danger, uncertainty, and hope, stood in the yard with its team hitched. It was a less laden wagon than had come north. Thomas and Blue-Jay alone were retracing their path.

They had waited as long as possible to begin the journey, helping with the house that Ian Cameron had gone back to raising. But the End of Fruit Moon was waning, the nights lengthening, leaving behind a hint of autumn to greet them on the morning air. It would not be many more weeks before snow whitened the mountains of their home, and the journey was far. He and his son had spoken of it the night before as they lay down to sleep beneath the arbor.

"Are you sure, Edo'da?" Blue-Jay had asked. "You will not return with me?"

"I am too old to make that journey again." Runs-Far gazed out at the stars glittering in the black of night as he spoke. "I wish to spend what is left of my days with Chickadee...Lily...and her family, to know them as I know you and Redwing. For that I will need all the time that is left to me, short or long."

Thomas was going back to his work of guiding slaves to freedom, with the aid of John Reynold, Ambrose Kincaid—and Ian Cameron. Runs-Far thought the chances were good he would be seeing that one again.

"At the very least," Thomas said now as he and Ian shook hands in the cabin yard, "I mean to return the wagon team to John. I'll be back eventually, with any parcels he might have to send your way—of whatever sort."

After other farewells were spoken—to Seona and her family, to Naomi and Ally and Esther, who had found her home with them—Blue-Jay and Runs-Far stood alone with Chickadee. Runs-Far took from the bag at his side the moccasins he had carried from Thunder-Going-Away's Town.

"I have waited long to give these to you. They were made by your mother's hands." He held them out to this youngest child.

She took them, cradling them on her palms like tiny birds. "My mama made these?"

"As soon as she knew you were there in her belly, growing."

"They're beautiful." Chickadee's lips trembled. She pressed the moccasins to them.

"It will be your daughter who wears them," Blue-Jay said. "Your Jemma."

Chickadee smiled through her tears. "I've no words deep enough or wide enough to speak my heart." Holding tight to the moccasins, she threw her arms around Runs-Far and held him, then did the same to Blue-Jay, who she released with reluctance. "I don't want ye to go. Not so soon."

Voice husky, Blue-Jay said, "But I go to our sister, to tell her of you. Of all these here."

Chickadee nodded. She had asked many questions about Redwing, their village, their lives, as had Seona. "Will ye come back to us?"

It was a thing no man could rightly know—what the future held. "If I can."

"One day I would see all my children together, standing on the earth in front of my eyes," Runs-Far said. "If Creator wills it."

"Aye," Chickadee said. "God willing."

In one of the cabins both babies started up a hungry crying. Chickadee touched her brother's arm, crossed the yard to Seona, and the two went inside to tend to their children. And no doubt to admire the work of his Walnut's hands.

Thomas sat on the wagon's bench, talking with Ian Cameron, out of earshot of their voices. Time had come for this hardest parting. "I would tell you a thing, my son. A thing Ian told me after the wedding dance."

Blue-Jay's eyes, his mother's amber, welled with tears. "What is it, Edo'da?"

"Before your sister and her daughter came here to be with him, Ian had a vision from Creator of all those whom he wished to love and nurture—those with white skin like his, and the red-brown skin of our people, and the dark brown skin of those his kin once enslaved—gathered in this place to live in freedom and peace." Runs-Far swallowed hard, smiling at his son. "That dance we led at his sister's wedding felt to him like a fulfillment of that vision, all of us joined by the hands around one fire, moving with the same steps. That is what he said to me."

Tears rolled down Blue-Jay's cheeks. "Those are good words, Edo'da, and I am not so small-minded I cannot admit I was wrong about that one. Ian Cameron has a good heart. But that dance ... it was one night. Many are leaving again, going separate ways. Malcolm will soon be leaving. *I* am leaving."

Runs-Far raised a hand to grip his son's arm, where Chickadee had touched it last. He felt the strength beneath his fingers, the years still to be lived. "That is all true. Malcolm has reached the end of his days. And it is your path, for now, to go from this place. But let me remind you of a thing you know in your heart. For you and me, for all who love Creator-Jesus and are remade in Him, there is no final parting. We will meet again, in this life or the next, and it will be then as I sung for the dance. Every tribe. Every people. We will all stand together in the Light and sing."

Blue-Jay nodded. He did not seem able now to speak.

"But if you can return to us," Runs-Far added, "you will always have a home with this part of your clan. As would Redwing or her children. Any who may come. For now, go and tell them of these ones here—as you promised to do."

The amber eyes so like his Walnut's widened. "Did Redwing tell you I made that promise?"

Runs-Far nodded. "She waits for you to keep it."

They clasped each other's arm, then Blue-Jay climbed onto the wagon bench beside Thomas Ross. There were final waves, good-byes called from young and old across the farm, then the wagon wheels began turning.

"It's a long way to travel," Ian said, coming to stand beside Runs-Far. "Just the two of them. D'ye think ... will he be all right, Blue-Jay? Not too lonely?"

Runs-Far thought about that as the wagon rolled away. "One can never know who Creator will bring across one's path on such a journey. Those in need. Those ready to supply a need." Faces crossed his memory, all the ones they had encountered, each with their part to play in guiding him on this journey that had seen the healing of hearts and, at the last, the miracle of a daughter, this place, and all who called it home. "Who can say? My son may come to like this journeying back and forth, as your friend Thomas seems to do."

Beside him Ian laughed, as Esther's wolf-dog came from wherever it had been and thrust its nose beneath his hand. "There's every chance of it, Grandfather—if it's a catching thing."

Runs-Far watched the wagon carrying his son away until the trees along the track to Shiloh, and the world beyond, swallowed it. Then he returned the gaze of the man who had married his granddaughter and was working to build this place for her to live. For all of them to live. As his vision had guided him to do.

Naomi and Esther stepped from their cabin, heading toward the place where the chickens were kept. The wolf-dog bounded after them. The sound of hammering up at the house started, where Ian's father and Ally had gone to work.

"It will be a good day," Runs-Far said, "when we see that wagon coming back along that track, whoever it comes bearing."

"It will," Ian agreed, and went to join the building, leaving Runs-Far standing in the cabin yard, listening to the life of that place happening around him.

Seona's children were laughing with their grandmother, off among the beeches. He did not know where Joseph was. Maybe in the stable, seeing to horses. Or off starting on the cabin where he and Chickadee and little Jemma would live.

More laughter issued from the open door of the cabin where the mothers tended their infants. There was the brief sound of a nursing baby breaking off to give a fretful cry—new life—and a faint snore from the other cabin. A life soon to pass into eternity. Time moving in its circle.

"They are yours, as much as any of them are mine," Runs-Far said to no one he could see with his eyes. Recalling the vision that had begun his journey, he smiled. In his mind Walnut no longer scolded. She smiled too. As for his light... he thought it would remain on the earth yet awhile, for he had found again his first love, his deep love, for Creator.

Runs-Far returned to the cabin where the babies had been named. He pulled a stool across the floor to sit by Malcolm's bed. When the older man woke, they would talk of the long road each had taken to that place. They would speak of what that road had taught them of walking with Creator-Jesus.

And they would tell each other of the ones who would be waiting, once they reached their journey's end.

Author's Note and Acknowledgements

The Journey of Runs-Far concludes the Kindred series, comprising the novel *Mountain Laurel* and its sequel, *Shiloh* (both published by Tyndale House Publishers). Most of you have probably come to this story after reading those two books. Some may have read all the books this novella harkens back to, many of my previously published novels set amidst the sprawling eighteenth century world I've woven book by book, over the past decade. If that's you, I hope you found this story the richer for it and enjoyed the peek into the future lives of some of my earlier novels' characters. If you haven't read my previous books but would like to, see this novella's front matter for a list of titles. Also indicated are the characters Runs-Far and Blue-Jay met and in which title you will find their stories told. For instance, if you want more of Joanna and Alex MacKinnon's story (and Runs-Far and Jemma's), read *The King's Mercy.* You'll find Jesse and Tamsen's story in *The Pursuit of Tamsen Littlejohn.* For more on Ian Cameron and Seona, begin with *Mountain Laurel.*

While this novella has been an independently published effort—my first—I've been at this writing and publishing business long enough to have learned the value of a skilled and insightful editor. For this book, that was Julee Schwarzburg, who is due my thanks for spotting the early manuscript's weak and confusing passages (hopefully rectified), as well as its strengths. Thank you, Julee! Much of what I end up liking best about my novels emerges during its editing. This story is no exception.

I have both Tyndale House and fellow author and artist Roseanna White to thank for a cover that, in my agent's words, "feels like a Kindred book." I so agree!

Thank you, Wendy Lawton, and the rest of the Books & Such Literary Management team, for making the existence of this novella a possibility. Most particularly, my thanks to Ginny Smith, who shepherded this project, and me, through the daunting process of self-publishing from beginning to end.

And last but never least, thank you, readers, for embracing Ian and Seona and the rest of the Kindred series characters, for talking about these books and posting reviews online, and for letting me know how the journeys these characters have taken have touched or moved you. Hopefully you've found this conclusion to the series a satisfying one. I'd love to hear from you about it. You can contact me (and learn more about my historical novels) on my website at Loribenton.com or find me on Facebook @AuthorLoriBenton.

As always, I wish you happy reading!

About the Author

LORI BENTON was raised in Maryland, with generations-deep roots in southern Virginia and the Appalachian frontier. Her historical novels transport readers to the eighteenth century, where she expertly brings to life the colonial and early federal periods of North American history. Her books have received the Christy Award and the Inspy Award and have been honored as finalists for the ECPA Book of the Year. Lori is most at home surrounded by mountains, currently those of the Pacific Northwest, where, when she isn't writing, she's likely to be found in wild places behind a camera.

Made in the USA
Middletown, DE
20 November 2021